"This second volume of King's KD Thorne series is a ballet of tension and rough justice. A journalistic lens captures small-town America's downward slide.... and the author's winning agents go big to prove they can't be trifled with....A trim, gripping, casually brutal small-town epic."—*Kirkus Reviews*

A few fingers sticking up out of freshly dug dirt...

After an undercover FBI agent working for an interagency taskforce is found dead in a county park, National Defense Agency operatives KD Thorne and Jeffery Blunt are sent to Mercy Creek, Iowa, to run a parallel investigation into drug running, gun smuggling, and police corruption.

Who's running the guns and trafficking the drugs? How was the undercover agent discovered? Which cops can be trusted and how many are on the take?

As KD and Blunt follow the money trail and contraband up and down Interstate 35 from Iowa to south Texas, the traffickers push back, eager to protect their anonymity and their business. Will KD and Blunt unravel the conspiracy before the traffickers find the opportunity to put them in their graves?

Murder at Mercy Creek is a swiftly paced thriller that will keep you reading into the night. If you like unpredictable plot twists and nail-biting suspense, you'll love the second novel in the KD Thorne series.

MURDER AT MERCY CREEK

A KD THORNE THRILLER

MICHAEL P. KING

Blurred Lines Press

Murder at Mercy Creek

Michael P. King

ISBN 978-1-952711-09-1

Cover design by Paramita Bhattacharjee at creativeparamita.com

Always for Sarah

1

I n the morning, early, before the frost melted, Grace Abernathy
was walking her collie off leash in Peterbo County Park just
outside Mercy Creek, Iowa, on the wooded path that ran all the
way back to the far west end of the park, near the county maintenance sheds. The dog had gotten way ahead of her, and he wasn't
supposed to be off leash. She looked off into the brush on both sides
of the path. "Jeffie," she called.

In the distance to her right, she saw him over by the sheds,
digging near the mulch piles. She kept calling, but he paid no attention. She was going to have to go get him before a county employee
spotted him.

"Come on now, get out of that," she said. The dirt was loose where
he was digging, and the hole was already six or seven inches deep.
She glanced around to make sure they were alone before she grabbed
him by the collar and attached his leash. As she pulled him away
from the hole, she noticed what looked like two human fingers
wearing red nail polish peeking up through the dirt. She bent down
for a better look, felt dizzy, and sat down on the ground, her hand on
her chest. She breathed in and out, trying to get her breathing under

control for what seemed like a long time before she finally felt herself enough to call 911.

THE FIRST TEAGUE COUNTY sheriff's deputy on the scene called Henry Granger, the CEO of R&G Construction, before he called the sheriff. Granger, standing at the sink in his bathroom, wiped the shaving cream off his acne-scarred face and then answered his cell phone. He listened to the deputy without speaking and then ended the call.

His wife, still in her silk pajamas, poked her head into the bathroom with a cup of coffee in her hand. "Anything wrong?"

"Just business," he replied. "I need the room."

She set the coffee on the sink counter. "I'll go get dressed."

Granger tapped his phone on the side of the sink. Maybe there was still time. He called Teague County Sheriff James Crowder's personal cell phone. "We've got a problem."

"We don't have a problem. You've got a problem."

"Nobody knows yet."

"That retired lady knows. And by the way, if anything happens to her, all bets are off."

"So you won't cover this up?"

"I can't cover this up. I can spin it, but that's about it. So strap your helmet on."

By lunchtime the find was on cable news. Five dead in a mass grave. Granger sat in his Escalade in the parking lot of the R&G Construction facilities talking with Mateo Smits, his right-hand man.

"This is unacceptable."

"I know, Henry. We'd narrowed the snitches down to that group. We worked them. Nobody told us anything. Then Chris accidentally killed the girl. After that, there was no turning back."

"I was counting on you to deal with this personally."

"With all due respect, you told me to get Crowder's son out of there and make sure he got home, so that's what I did."

"Find out who dug that hole. Have them dig a deeper hole and put them in it."

"Yes, sir."

"Go on."

He watched Smits walk across the parking lot and get into his truck. There was no reason to put it off any longer. He took a burner phone out of his glove box and made a call to Nuevo Laredo, Mexico.

"Henry, I've been waiting to hear from you."

"I wanted to have all the facts, Mr. Juarez."

"And do you have the facts?"

"A reliable guy is dealing with the error."

"Do you even know if one of them was the informant?"

"It had to be one of them."

"We partnered with you in the US because you had a plan to move our product without attracting attention. But now we're beginning to wonder if we made the right choice. You lost a shipment of guns. Okay, that could happen. Can't buy off every cop. But something as basic as getting rid of a few bodies?"

"Those idiots are being dealt with."

"I hope so. I hope the example will be fixed in everyone's mind."

"It will."

"No more mistakes. No more publicity. Or we'll have to revisit our arrangement." Mr. Juarez ended the call.

Granger set the burner phone down on the console between the seats. *Revisit our arrangement.* That was an interesting euphemism. All R&G profits came from moving drugs and guns up and down the I-35 corridor. The construction contracts in Oklahoma and Texas gave them the cover to drive semitrucks north and south without attracting any attention. Underbidding the contracts guaranteed they'd win the jobs. And hiring construction crews was an easy introduction to the local sheriffs and elected officials, most all of whom could be bribed at one level or another—maybe with something as simple as election cash or jobs for family. It was a well-oiled machine. It would be easier for the Mexicans to replace him than to upset the system. Granger looked at his watch. The call had been too short to trace, but he pulled the chip from the phone and snapped in in half anyway. From here on out, he was going to double down on security.

. . .

JIMMY CROWDER, lanky and bearded, was driving a R&G semitruck loaded with construction materials down Interstate 35, heading toward Eagle Grove, Oklahoma. It was a good day for driving. No rain. A little overcast. The traffic moving at a steady pace. The new Waxahachie album on his Spotify. His phone buzzed. It was a text from Roslyn, his girlfriend. *Call me when you're not driving.* What could that be about? She couldn't be pregnant. He'd already agreed to move in with her. Maybe she'd found a little house to rent. But why couldn't they talk about that while he was driving? She was always wanting his complete attention.

He pulled off at a rest stop, one of the old ones that was just restrooms and a soda machine. Only two other tractor-trailer rigs were parked in the truck lanes. When he climbed down out of the cab, the air felt sticky outside. He crossed the drive lane to the restrooms, and on the way back he stopped under a tree by a picnic table to call Roslyn.

"Hey," he said.

"Are you driving?" Her voice sounded shaky.

"No. I'm at a rest stop."

"Has your dad called you?"

"No. What's up?"

"Have you heard any news?"

"Honey, I've been driving all day. What's going on?"

"Pat and Susan, Mike, Billy, and Philip—they were all murdered."

"What are you talking about?"

"I'm not kidding. Old lady's dog dug them up out by the county maintenance sheds at Peterbo Park this morning."

"That can't be right. I saw all of them last night at around eleven thirty or so."

"It's them, Jimmy. Their parents IDed them. It's all over the news."

"It's got to be a mistake."

She started crying. "It's no mistake. Call your dad." She ended the call.

He speed-dialed his dad's personal phone, but it went directly to voice mail. This didn't make any sense at all. They were always together when he wasn't at work or out with Roslyn. He found his dad's work number.

"Sheriff's department."

"Lisa, I need to talk to my dad."

"I'm so sorry about your friends, Jimmy. I'll put you through."

"Sheriff Crowder speaking."

"Dad? Roslyn just called me."

"You at work?"

"I'm in Missouri. Why didn't you call me?"

"It's been crazy around here. Were you out with all of them last night?"

"Out at the Payne's farm pond."

"When did you see them last?"

"About eleven thirty. Mateo collected me, said Mr. Granger needed me early this morning."

"And he dropped you at home?"

"Yeah. Another guy drove my truck."

"And you didn't see your friends after that?"

"Dad, is it really them?"

"Yes."

"It isn't possible there's been some mistake?"

"No. Their faces were recognizable."

"And they were buried out in Peterbo Park?"

"Looks like a gang killing."

"They didn't have anything to do with gangs."

"I know."

"I just can't get my mind around it."

"You get home tonight?"

"Late."

"Drive careful."

"Something's got to be done, Dad."

"We're doing it. Everything we can."

Jimmy wiped his eyes on the sleeve of his shirt. It just couldn't be.

He'd wake up in a few minutes. A semitruck rolling by on the inter-state blasted its horn. He couldn't remember saying goodbye, and now he'd never see them again. He could see all their faces sitting around the fire. Just another night at the pond. He shook his head. He needed to deliver this load and get home.

OUTSIDE WASHINGTON, DC, at the Suitland headquarters of the National Defense Agency, Assistant Director Clara Garcia, a full-figured woman who favored black pantsuits accented by a small gold cross on a chain, sat in her office on the phone with FBI Special Agent-in-Charge Jerome Victor of the Counter Terrorist Taskforce.

"Did you see the news out of Mercy Creek, Iowa?" Victor asked.

"Hard to miss it. You lose one of yours?"

"Yes. A talented undercover. He was just starting to make progress."

"You've got my condolences. But why are we talking?"

"We did some good work together on that terrorism case a few years back."

"The Persian carpet case?"

"That's the one. We could use your help here."

"Go on."

"This was not just some drug gang killing. The FBI, DEA, and ATF have been coordinating on a corruption probe of cities running up Interstate 35 from south Texas into Iowa. Three regional federal law enforcement supervisors have taken early retirement. Now an FBI undercover has been murdered. We know the cartel is moving drugs and guns—that's nothing new. But we don't know how far the corruption goes. Is it individual law enforcement? Or whole depart-ments, city officials, members of state legislatures? That's what we're trying to find out. But every time we start to make progress, we hit a roadblock."

"And you're afraid you've got a mole inside your investigation."

"Exactly. You're on the outside. Can you send in a team to run a parallel investigation?"

"My people will have to handle things their own way."

"Of course."

"Email me what you have."

CAPTAIN KD THORNE and Warrant Officer Jeffery Blunt, dressed in gym shorts, T-shirts, and military boots, were running down a trail in a wooded section along the water in Rock Creek Park in Washington, DC. KD was moving fast, her long braid swinging across her back in time to her stride. Blunt, a black man about ten years her senior, all hard muscle and sweat, was following about six feet behind.

KD called back over her shoulder. "You're huffing and puffing, old man. You going to make the full five miles, or do I need to call a medivac?"

"You are so funny, Doc. Maybe you should go to open mic night. Somebody start shooting, you'll see me pick up my game."

"I'll bring a gun next time."

They came out of the woods and ran along the road. The parking lot for the police substation was directly ahead of them. "Don't we turn around here?" Blunt asked.

KD nodded. They circled around in the parking lot to start back.

Blunt chuckled.

"What's so funny?"

"That guy across the road reminded me of your pool boy."

"He's not a pool boy, Blunt. He's a personal trainer at my gym. Got to be at least thirty. And I'm not chasing him. Just chatting him up a little."

"How does your husband feel about that?"

"Ex-husband."

"You ain't been acting like he's your ex."

"We've been having some fun times; I won't deny it. But I don't owe Frank anything."

"Uh-huh."

"What?"

"Then why you feeling guilty?"

"I'm not feeling guilty."

"Then why won't you tell him he's got competition?"

She felt her phone vibrate in her pocket and checked her messages. "Garcia wants us."

"Let's take the shortcut back."

Two hours later, KD and Blunt, freshly showered and dressed in dark suits, sat across from Garcia in her government regulation office. The US president and the head of the National Defense Agency stared down on them from their pictures on the wall behind her.

"There wasn't much in the FBI taskforce report," KD said. "Their undercover—Philip Richards—was just getting started. They busted a load of guns headed for Mexico. Three weeks later, Richards is dead. Pretty much all we know is that this cartel runs a tight ship. They had a leak and they patched it. But we don't know where they got their information from."

"So you'll have to start there," Garcia said.

"Can we get the ATF and the DEA reports?" Blunt asked.

Garcia shook her head. "Everybody's pointing fingers, blaming the other agencies for any possible leaks."

"Then I guess we're starting from scratch," Blunt said.

"The way in is through these murders, but the job's not just finding out who killed the undercover. The job's about finding out the extent of the corruption from the Texas border up through Iowa, which officials have been bought off, and what they're doing for the cartel."

"We're on it, boss," KD said.

AT LUNCHTIME THE NEXT DAY, Sheriff Crowder and Henry Granger sat at a booth in Poppa Joe's Diner. The booths and the stools at the counter were all occupied, and several people stood in the doorway, waiting for a table. The waitresses, dressed in jeans and Poppa Joe's T-shirts, were hustling down the aisles. The blue-plate special was meatloaf, mashed potatoes, and green beans. The sheriff swallowed a mouthful of meatloaf before he leaned forward to keep his voice down, his beer belly rubbing against the table and the overhead light shining off his shaved head. "No one will give you cover on this. The state wants a look, the Feds want a look."

"My friends have assured me that nothing else is going to happen," Granger replied. "Drag your feet. People will lose interest."

"You sure about that? Five kids, for Christ's sake."

"I kept your son out of it."

"I know. I appreciate it."

"How's he doing?"

"He's all busted up about it."

"Is that a problem?"

"No. He'll keep his mouth shut. Besides, he doesn't know anything."

"Then it's business as usual."

"There's only so much I can do. Three city council members have already called me."

"They'll stop whining when it's the end of the month and they have their hands out."

"I'm just saying—"

"Don't worry. We'll give you something juicy before the next election. Just do your job. Reassure everyone. You'll make a drug bust next week, arrest some farmer's kid at a meth lab. It's all going to be fine."

"I hope you're right."

After they finished eating, the sheriff made a show of leaving his own tip and paying for his own meal at the cash register.

They pushed through the glass doors out into the noontime glare. "Did you really need to do that?" Granger asked.

"Can't be too careful," the sheriff replied. "Need to look like I'm my own man."

"Your son's across the street."

The sheriff squinted. His son Jimmy was leaning against the driver's door of his departmental Ford Explorer.

"See you later," the sheriff said. He glanced both ways before he crossed the street.

Jimmy Crowder stood up from the Explorer. His eyes were red-rimmed and his clothes were wrinkled. "Are you trying to avoid me, Dad?"

"No, I'm not. I've been busy. I've got all my usual work plus—you know."

"But you've got time to eat lunch with Mr. Granger."

The sheriff motioned for Jimmy to move away from the driver's side door. "Get in the truck."

Once they were both in the front seats, Jimmy continued. "All my friends, murdered. I heard they were tortured. That Susan was raped."

"All conjecture until the state lab report comes back."

"What are you going to do about it?"

"When did you get back in town?"

"Last night."

"We've got a full investigation underway."

"Why? You know who did it."

"No, I don't. And you don't either. We can't just run off half-cocked."

"That's bullshit. R&G must have thought they had something to do with the load of weapons that got confiscated."

"Do you have any proof? Did you see anything, hear anything, find anything to support your claim? That's the way the law works. Proof. Where did you sleep last night?"

"I was at Roslyn's."

"Have you seen your mother? She's worried sick. Pat was like a son to her."

"Are you going to do your job?"

"We're going to follow the evidence and arrest the killers. You need to settle down and keep your mouth shut."

AT 11:30 P.M., in a room at the Hyatt Hotel in downtown Washington, DC, KD Thorne lay on the queen-size bed beside her ex-husband Frank, their hands clasped together. She glanced at him in the dark, his hard body and tousled red hair. He usually came into town about once a month to do lobbying for Volstagg Engineering, and when he did, they went out to dinner and back to his hotel room.

She let out a deep breath. "That was good."

He squeezed her hand.

"But the beard is scratchy."

"You want me to shave it off?"

"It's your face, honey."

He leaned over and kissed her. "Can you stay the night?"

"I'm leaving on a job in a day or two, so I've got to be in the office early."

"How long will you be gone?"

"Don't know. I'll text you when I get back."

"It's that kind of job?"

"Uh-huh."

"A lot different from doing research at NASA."

She glanced at the clock on the night table. "Didn't realize it was so late." She rolled off the bed and padded across the carpet into the bathroom. When she came out, she went to the chair where her clothes lay and started getting dressed in the light from the open bathroom door.

"Want me to take you home?" he asked.

"No need. I'll get a ride share."

After she put on her sports coat, she walked around to Frank's side of the bed and leaned down to kiss him. "See you next month, if I'm back."

He scooted up in bed. "This is going to break the mood—thought we could talk about it in the morning—but I've got to ask you a question."

"That's your serious voice."

"Maybe I'm paranoid, but I'm just getting the feeling that maybe you're looking for another guy."

"I don't owe you any explanation."

"So that's how it's going to be."

"You're the one who divorced me."

"I know."

"You're the one who decided that was a mistake."

"I know."

"Are you having a good time?"

"You know what I mean, Katie. It's frustrating that I don't know what I've got to do to win back your trust."

"It is frustrating. I don't know either. Maybe it's not possible."

"Don't say that."

"I care about you, Frank. Otherwise, I wouldn't be here. But I can't promise anything. Look, it's late. I don't want to get into this now. I'll see you when I get back."

She started down the hall to the elevator. The mess that was her life. Why couldn't she see her way through? She wanted a real relationship. A relationship like the one she'd thought she'd had with Frank before the divorce. They were good together. Had history together. Could almost finish each other's sentences. They'd fallen into—what would you call it? Friends with benefits? No, it was more than that. But the pain of being rejected by him, the man she'd loved, was still smoldering inside her. She just couldn't seem to let it go. Maybe she would be better off with someone else. She pressed the button for the elevator. It would be good to be back in the field. That was the only place where everything made sense.

2

Two days later, in the late afternoon, KD and Blunt drove over the bridge on Johnson Boulevard into Mercy Creek, Iowa, in a tan Camry they'd rented at the Des Moines airport. The downtown looked worn and rundown, a number of storefronts needed facelifts, and about a quarter of the stores had *For Lease* signs in their windows.

"Hardware store, drugstore, bank, Dollar Store, two restaurants, gun shop—that's about it," Blunt said.

KD flipped through NDA Agent Tina Han's report. "Yeah, but this town is bigger than it looks downtown. There's two chain grocery stores, a couple of strip malls, a Walmart, and the mall out by the freeway."

"The parking lot at the mall was about half empty."

"It's a weekday." She turned to a section on page four. "Large number of overdose deaths, especially compared to the number of drug arrests. Town didn't recover from the last recession. They'd really be hurting if R&G Construction hadn't set up a warehouse facility here."

Blunt parked in front of the county jail. They went in through the front door and stopped at the counter before the metal detector. The female deputy behind the counter glanced at them from behind the plexiglass. KD took out her ID and set it on the counter. "The sheriff is expecting us."

The deputy read the ID. "One moment." She picked up her desk phone and pressed an extension button. "Sheriff? The National Defense Agency people are here."

She turned back to KD and Blunt. "You armed?"

They nodded.

"You'll have to leave your weapons here."

They each checked the safeties on their SIG Sauer M18 pistols and then passed them through the slot in the plexiglass.

"Come on." She walked them around the metal detector and down the hallway to the sheriff's office.

Sheriff Crowder was standing behind his desk. "Have a seat." He indicated the two chairs facing his desk.

"Sheriff," KD said, "I'm Agent Thorne and this is Agent Blunt."

"Don't believe I've ever met any of you NDA people before." The sheriff leaned back in his chair. "What can I do for you?"

"We're looking into the Peterbo Park murders."

"I didn't think the NDA did murder investigations."

"We don't. We've looking into possible terrorist connections."

"Terrorists? Why would terrorists be here in Teague County?"

"We aren't saying there are terrorists. We're just looking into it. You wouldn't call five bodies in a mass grave your usual sort of murder, would you?"

"I wouldn't call any murder in this county usual."

Blunt continued. "Have you got any leads?"

"Not yet. It's early. All the physical evidence is at the state lab. It can take a while to get the results back."

"What do you know about the victims?"

"Just local kids. No records. Friends of my son, actually. Just a group of kids taking too long to grow up."

"Your son must be taking it hard."

"Yeah, it's tough. They all came up together."

"Can we get a look at the crime scene?" KD asked.

"Sure. I'll take you out there myself."

They followed the sheriff's Explorer down a state highway, rolling past corn and soybean fields that were golden dry and ready for harvest. At the northwest perimeter of Peterbo Park, they pulled off the highway at a county road maintenance equipment storage site and parked on the gravel between a gray, sheet-metal equipment shed and a twenty-foot-high wood mulch pile. Nearby was an area cordoned off by police tape.

The sheriff walked them over to the police tape, where they all looked down into an excavated hole.

"What is that? Four feet? Wasn't very deep," Blunt said.

"No, it wasn't," the sheriff replied. He pointed to a wooded area to the south of the grave site. "That's Peterbo Park. An off-leash dog came over here, started digging, the owner came for the dog, saw a hand sticking out of the dirt."

"Why bury them here?" KD asked.

The sheriff pointed to the equipment shed. "They broke the lock on the shed, used a mini-digger to make the hole. Maybe it was just convenient."

"Fingerprints?" Blunt asked.

"No such luck," the sheriff replied.

KD gestured toward the row of houses across a soybean field to the east. "No one heard anything or saw anything?"

He shook his head. "We went door to door."

"But light from here would certainly have shown over at those houses."

"Headlights definitely. Flashlights maybe."

"And the digger had to make some kind of noise. Does the county work out here in the middle of the night?"

"Earliest might be 5:00 a.m."

KD looked back down in the hole. "So this wasn't the best choice."

"If the hole had been deeper, they might have gotten away with it."

"Where were the victims before they were brought here?" Blunt asked.

"Don't know. Around 11:30 p.m., they were out at a fishing pond on my cousin's farm. My son went home. We don't know what happened to the others after that."

"So your son was with them? What were they doing at a fishing pond at eleven o'clock at night?" KD asked.

The sheriff shrugged. "Drinking, smoking weed, looking at the sky. How the hell would I know?"

"Lucky break for your son," Blunt said.

"You're telling me."

"You all searched the area around the pond?"

"You know, I'm beginning to think you'd like to tell me my business."

"Just want all the details."

"Yeah, we searched. Nothing of interest. Still think it looks like terrorists?" the sheriff asked.

"Don't know," KD replied. "It's not a crime of passion. Nobody contacted the media, so it's not somebody making a statement. Beyond that, I don't have any idea what it is."

They walked back toward their vehicles.

"How long do you think you'll be in town?"

"I'm not sure. We have to do due diligence, file a report. So we'll talk with the parents and their friends, see if that leads anywhere."

"I've already done all that. You can have my report. It'll save you some time."

"I appreciate your cooperation, Sheriff, but your angle is the murders while ours is possible terrorism, so we may have different questions. We'll try to stay out of your way, and we'll share anything we find out, but that's the way it has to be. Thanks for bringing us out here."

The sheriff got into his Explorer and turned left out of the gravel parking lot. KD and Blunt got into the Camry, Blunt driving, turned right, and started down the highway toward town. "What do you think?" KD asked.

"He seemed a little too folksy to me," Blunt replied.

"And a little too helpful. Showing us around himself, offering his report, maybe he's just a great guy ..."

Blunt smiled. "Or maybe he just wants to get rid of us."

THAT EVENING GRANGER was waiting for the sheriff behind the high school in the parking lot next to the tennis courts. The sheriff parked his SUV in a dark spot between streetlights, crossed over to Granger's Escalade, and climbed in the passenger seat.

"What took you so long?" Granger asked. "I've been waiting here twenty minutes."

"Had to finish supper."

Granger grunted. "I heard about the federal agents."

"Is that why you wanted to meet? Nothing to worry about," the sheriff replied. "They're not law enforcement."

"Then what are they?"

"National Defense Agency investigators."

"What did they want?"

"Looking for terrorist connections to the murders."

"Does that sound right to you?"

"Don't know. But they won't find out anything, so it doesn't matter."

"Get rid of them."

"I wish I could. But if I try to pressure them, they're going to dig in their heels. The best plan is the wait them out."

"You sure they can't find out anything?"

"Who knows anything?"

Granger nodded. "Okay. Keep me informed."

"You bet."

The sheriff went back to his SUV and drove off. Granger reached into his glovebox for a burner phone. "Mateo? The one loose end taken care of?"

"Yes, Henry."

"There were three others?"

"That's right."

"Send them on vacation to Mexico. Tell them we'll let them know when it's safe to come back."

"Gotcha."

"And Mateo? They leave in the morning."

THE NEXT DAY, KD and Blunt set out to interview the parents of the victims. Their first stop was Helen and Joseph Green, Pat Green's parents. They lived in a well-cared-for ranch house on a quiet street of similar houses. All their neighbors who were out in the yards or on the porches looked to be of retirement age. KD and Blunt parked on the street in front of the Green residence, walked up the sidewalk and rang the doorbell.

A man wearing a white, V-neck T-shirt, a gray fringe of hair circling his head, answered the door.

"Mr. Green?" KD showed her ID. "I'm Agent Thorne and this is Agent Blunt. We're with the National Defense Agency. We'd like to ask you a few questions about your son, Pat."

"Sure, come in." As he led them to the living room, he called toward the kitchen. "Helen, we've got company."

A silver-haired woman wearing yoga clothes came in from the kitchen.

"Government people," Mr. Green said. "Want to know about Pat."

"Sit down," Helen said.

KD and Blunt sat on the sofa. The Greens sat down in two armchairs across the coffee table and then looked at them expectantly.

KD started. "I'm sorry for your loss. Must be quite a shock."

Helen nodded. "It's still not really believable."

"I've got some questions I need to ask. Anything you can tell me would be a help."

They nodded.

"I understand that Pat, Susan, Mike, Billy, and Philip grew up together."

"Not Philip," Mr. Green said. "The others all met in kindergarten. He showed up last winter. Isn't that right, Helen?"

"And Jimmy," she said. "They were all close friends."

"The sheriff's son?" KD said.

"That's right."

"But only Philip was new?"

"Yes. He was a good boy, but that's right. He was new."

"Where did Pat work?"

"Pat drove trucks for R&G Construction," Mr. Green said. "Jimmy got him the job."

"Did he like truck driving?"

"Well enough. Good jobs are hard to come by here."

"And he still lived at home?"

"Saving up to buy a house. He and Susan were going to get married."

"What did she do?"

"She cut hair at Any Cuts, out at the mall."

"What about the others?"

"Mike worked at the Hy-Vee grocery and Billy—what was he doing, dear?"

"Wasn't he taking classes to become an electrician?" Helen replied.

Mr. Green nodded. "That's right."

"Had Pat seemed uneasy lately?" KD continued. "Out of sorts? Worried about anything?"

They shook their heads.

"Had his patterns changed?"

"No. The kids all hung out together, did everything together, just like they had ever since high school."

Helen started to sniffle. "It's so hard. Just when he was finally finding his way. Will we ever know why?"

"I don't know, Mrs. Green, but we'll try to find out."

"It was a mistake," Mr. Green said. "Had to be. Wrong place, wrong time."

"Do you know where he'd been the night before."

"No idea. Just out with the others. They were always together."

"If you think of anything else, give me a call." She left her card on the coffee table.

KD and Blunt walked back down the sidewalk to the Camry. Blunt pulled the fob from his pocket and unlocked the doors. "Doesn't make any sense, does it?"

"Not yet."

"Just regular kids doing the stupid stuff they do until they grow up."

"Hit a nerve?"

"It's a worrisome time for a parent, Doc. You want your kids to succeed, whatever that means, but they've got to run the gauntlet of car wrecks, drug ODs, idiot friends, and fantasy professions until their brains finally mature."

"Worried about your kids?"

"My kids are doing fine, so far as I know, but you don't know what you don't know." He started the car. "Who's next?"

"How about Susan Grisel's mother? She's out at the care center."

They drove out past the shopping mall to the other side of the freeway, where Sunny Oaks Manor was located. It was a tan brick, one story building with two wings coming off on either side of the entrance. They parked in the visitor parking.

"I'm already depressed," Blunt said.

"Some of these places are nice," KD replied.

"*Some* being the operative word."

"Where's your mom?"

"My folks have both passed a long time ago. What about you?"

"My dad lives in a retirement community in Florida. He's still in good shape."

"So he must be a popular guy with the widows."

"Don't start, Blunt."

"Just saying, Doc."

At the front desk, they asked for Mrs. Grisel. The receptionist called her room. "You can go down. E14."

They strolled down the east hallway. Most of the doors were open. At E14, Blunt knocked on the doorframe. "Mrs. Grisel?"

"Come in."

A tiny, white-haired woman wearing a light blue housecoat lay on a motorized bed, her head raised so that she could watch the TV hanging from the ceiling.

"Mrs. Grisel," KD said, "I'm Agent Thorne and this is Agent Blunt. We'd like to ask you some questions about your daughter."

Mrs. Grisel turned off the TV. "It's about time someone decided to do something."

"We're sorry for your loss."

"That's what everyone says."

"Do you know where Susan was the night before she was found?"

"No. I hadn't seen her since Sunday. She visits on Sunday and Wednesday."

"Must be a terrible shock."

"Not really. I told her she'd come to no good hanging around with that ne'er-do-well, Pat Green. That boy never had a lick of sense, not him or any of his friends. Wasted her life chasing after him." She pulled a tissue from the box on her night table. "Could have had any of the boys in high school. But she wasted herself on that trash." She dabbed at her eyes.

"Why did you disapprove of him?"

"Not even average. His parents spoiled him. He couldn't keep a job. It's one thing to gad about town if your father's the sheriff, but being the sheriff's son's best friend doesn't get you the key to the city. He should have married my daughter instead of stringing her along. And now she's dead."

"Your daughter worked as a hair stylist?"

"At Any Cuts, in the mall."

"Did she like working there?"

"I guess. Better than checking at the Casey's General Store."

"Did she have any problems with her boss or coworkers?"

"They don't murder you in the night for not getting along at work. They just fire you."

"So she came to visit on Sunday and Wednesday?"

"Every week."

"What did you talk about when she came to visit?"

"My shows. We watched the same TV shows. Her sister. You know, family stuff."

KD handed Mrs. Grisel her business card. "If you think of anything, give me a call."

Mrs. Grisel brought the card close to her face and squinted. "I won't."

KD and Blunt walked back down the hall to the entrance.

"Sounds like Susan was a complicated woman," KD said.

"Because the Greens said Pat was going to marry her, and her mom said he was leading her on? Mrs. Grisel could just be a bitter old woman," Blunt replied.

"I had an aunt that was like that—my mom's older sister—never satisfied, always assumed the worst in people."

"We still don't know who killed the undercover guy or why."

"Philip Richards? You don't think it was because the cartel was trying to root him out?"

"Probably was, but we don't have any evidence. We need to find out where they were at after they left the farm pond."

KD and Blunt interviewed Mike Belmont's parents and Billy Cannon's parents, but the story was the same. They didn't know where the group had ended up the night before. The kids were all finally settling down and accepting adult life. They weren't involved in anything illegal. Must have been plain bad luck.

After they pulled through the McDonald's drive-through, they parked under a tree in the corner of the parking lot to eat their lunch. Blunt took a sip of iced tea. "We going to try the workplaces next?"

"Let's think about this," KD replied. "Susan was a hair cutter. They're not going to know anything at the Any Cuts. Likewise, Cannon at the community college and Belmont at the grocery store. We could interview thirty people—"

"And hear some vague rumors that have nothing to do with our case," Blunt said. "But we've got reason to think R&G is involved, because their truck was busted carrying the guns."

"Exactly. So let's interview Pat's supervisor."

They drove over to the R&G warehouse complex. The gate in the chain-link fence was open. Three warehouses stood side by side, separated by ten-foot alleyways. They parked in the visitor parking spot in front of the door to the office located in the front of the first warehouse. To the right of the office, workers driving forklifts were loading construction materials onto four tractor-trailer rigs.

KD and Blunt went into the office. A full-figured older woman wearing jeans and a sweatshirt sat behind the counter.

"Can I help you?" she asked.

KD took out her ID. "I'm Agent Thorne and this is Agent Blunt. We're with the National Defense Agency. We're investigating the murders."

"Terrible thing," the woman said.

"Yes, ma'am. We'd like to speak to Pat Green's supervisor."

"That would be Mateo Smits. I'm not sure if he's here. Let me find out." She picked up a landline phone and punched an extension button. "Mateo here? Put him on."

A man in work clothes, his hands stained with grease, came into the office, glanced at KD and Blunt, and then sat down in a chair.

"Mateo?" The woman spoke into the phone. "Police are here with questions about Pat." She hung up and looked across the counter at KD. "He'll be here in a second."

"Thank you," KD said.

The woman turned to the man sitting in the chair and raised her eyebrows.

"The rigs are all loaded," he said.

"Your guys can take a break. There'll be a truck to unload in about twenty minutes."

The man nodded and left.

A dark-skinned Latino, dressed in jeans and cowboy boots, came in through an inner door. "You here to talk about Pat?"

"We've got some questions," KD said.

"Come on back."

He led them down a short hall to another office, where he sat behind a desk and gestured toward the two chairs facing him. They sat down.

"How can I help you?"

"Pat Green reported directly to you?" KD asked.

"Yes."

"How long had he worked here?"

Smits opened a laptop computer. "About six months."

"What were his duties?"

"Truck driver. Driving around town or long-haul down to Oklahoma or Texas or sometimes to Chicago."

"Carrying what?"

"Building materials, furnishings—we buy our materials direct from major wholesalers and run our own distribution chain. Very cost effective."

"Pat have any problems on the job?"

Smits shook his head. "Strong work record, reliable, on-time, easy personality—we're really going to miss him."

"So you've got no idea why he was murdered?"

"Complete surprise. Guy didn't have any enemies—at work, at least."

"Now, on the night in question, you went out to Payne's farm pond and picked up Jimmy Crowder?"

He nodded.

"Why?"

"We needed him driving an expedited load at 6:00 a.m. sharp."

"Sure, but why did you go get him? He's a grown man."

"Mercy Creek looks bigger than it is. But there's a lot of small town to it. R&G wants everything to run smoothly with the local government."

"Meaning?"

"We've just got to show respect, and part of that is hiring family of local officials and cutting them some slack if they do their jobs. Jimmy's a good worker. He's just not always on time. So if Mr.

Granger says make sure Jimmy's here first thing, rested and ready, I make sure."

"Must be a pain in the ass, playing nursemaid," Blunt said.

"Just part of my job."

"Who drove Jimmy's truck home?"

"Rudy Gomez."

"Can we talk to him if we need to?"

"Absolutely. If he's not on the road."

"Well, I think that covers it," KD said. She and Blunt stood up. "Thanks for your time."

"You bet."

"Oh," KD said, "one other thing. You had a truck stopped on the interstate a few weeks back. Illegal guns, wasn't it?"

"Guns were hidden in the load. We didn't know anything about it. A real embarrassment to our reputation, even though none of our people were charged."

"Think maybe the gangsters who did that are the same ones who killed Pat and his friends?"

"I don't have any idea."

"Well, thanks for your time."

KD and Blunt left the R&G warehouses, Blunt driving, and headed back toward their rooms at the Holiday Inn Express. "He didn't miss a beat, did he?"

"No, he had his story straight. Pat's a great guy, you have to play nice with the locals, the gun bust was a terrible embarrassment."

"Think he believed any of it?"

"I don't know," KD replied. "Maybe Pat Green was an all-around great guy."

"Maybe. But then why was he killed? Unless getting killed had nothing to do with his job."

"Which makes no sense. If the five friends had been doing dirt, someone would know something. And Philip Richards wouldn't have been in their crew if it didn't have something to do with his investigation. He gave the tip about the guns, the guns were interdicted, and three weeks later they were all murdered."

"Unless Smits really is as clueless as he claims to be."

Blunt took a right onto Johnson Boulevard and fell in behind a school bus. KD's phone rang. It was the sheriff. She put it on speaker.

"What can we do for you, Sheriff?"

"We got the report back from the state lab. They were all beaten pretty severely before they were shot. Susan had trauma consistent with sexual assault."

"No drugs?"

"Alcohol and marijuana."

"So it looks like they were being interrogated."

"Or made an example of."

"We talked with the parents. Nothing there."

"Like I said, I already interviewed them. This is my town. I'd know if these kids were doing anything seriously bad."

"Can we get a copy of the lab report?"

"Sure."

"By the way, we haven't had a chance to talk with your son yet. Do you know where he is?"

"He's not working, so if he isn't at home, he's probably at his girl-friend's." He gave them the address.

"Thanks." KD ended the call. She turned to Blunt. "You hear all that?"

Blunt nodded. "Labs just confirm what we thought." He glanced in the rearview mirror. "We've got a tail."

"Really?"

"Uh-huh. Black truck behind the red SUV. They're sloppy."

KD adjusted the rearview mirror so that she could see the truck without turning around in her seat. "Two Latinos."

"What do you want to do?"

"What can we do? If we ditch them, they'll just find us again. And then they'll know that we know."

"So, coincidence or a result of interviewing Smits?"

"I guess time will tell. Let's make a U-turn and see if we can find the sheriff's son."

. . .

Jimmy Crowder sat on the glider of the front porch of Roslyn's mom's Cape Cod style house, waiting for Roslyn to get home from work. He felt sick to his stomach. Usually, if he was in town, he'd be hanging out with whoever of the gang was already off work, maybe playing basketball down at the park or shooting pool at Scooter's Games. His phone rang. It was his dad.

"Report came back from the state lab. It's as bad as it can be."

"So they were tortured?"

"Yeah."

"And Susan was raped."

"Yeah."

"Damn it, Dad. Granger can't get away with this."

"Simmer down. How do you know it was him?"

"'Cause he's the boss."

"We've got to tread carefully here. You can't accuse them without any facts. If you stir up a bunch of trouble, how do you think we're going to find the evidence we need to solve this case? If you want justice, you need to shut up and go about your business."

"I won't wait forever."

"There's already too many fingers in this pie. National Defense Agency investigators showed up yesterday. They're looking for a terrorism connection."

"National Defense Agency? Who are they?"

"Federal agency. Not cops."

"Do you think that's true? You think maybe it was terrorists?"

"No. It's a big waste of time. But they've been interviewing everyone, and you're next. So keep your mouth shut. Give me a chance to find out who really killed your friends." The sheriff ended the call.

Jimmy put his phone back in his pants pocket. How could he wait? He had to do something. It wouldn't be long before people forgot about the murders. Rumors were already starting that Mike, Billy, and Pat were cooking meth, that they must have had it coming.

. . .

KD AND BLUNT parked in front of the house where Jimmy Crowder's girlfriend, Roselyn Billings, and her mother lived. A twenty-something man, slim and bearded, whose face bore a striking resemblance to the sheriff, was sitting on a glider on the porch. KD called up to him as she walked up the sidewalk. "Mr. Crowder? Jimmy Crowder?"

Jimmy stood up from the glider. "Yeah?"

"I'm Agent Thorne and this is Agent Blunt. Can we speak with you?"

"Are you the NDA investigators? My dad said you wanted to talk with me."

They climbed the steps to the porch. "May we sit?"

"Sure."

They sat down in the lawn chairs on either side of the glider.

"Sorry for your loss," KD said.

Jimmy shrugged.

"We've heard that you six were inseparable."

"That's right."

"Why weren't you with the others?"

"I was. We were all out at Payne's farm pond, north of town."

"But you left early?"

"I've been late getting to work, so my boss sent a couple of guys to get me."

"Who do you work for?"

"R&G. I drive a truck."

"And your boss sent someone to take you home?"

He rolled his eyes. "I'm the sheriff's son. They need to stay on the sheriff's good side, so they can't fire me for just being a little late. They wanted me fresh, first thing in the morning."

"Why didn't they just call you?"

"I'd had a few. I was waiting until I was safe to drive."

"Who came to get you?"

"Mateo Smits—he's my supervisor—and one of the guys."

"What time did they come for you?"

"After eleven thirty."

"Didn't Pat also drive for R&G?"

"Yeah, I recommended him."

Blunt continued. "So your boss collects you, and your friends get killed. That's a strange coincidence, don't you think?"

"I know. It's been eating me from the inside out. If I hadn't been late getting to work, if I wasn't the sheriff's son, I might be dead, too."

KD continued. "Did you often go out to the Payne's farm pond?"

"Yeah. They're our cousins. They don't live out there anymore, so we can go out whenever we want. We often go out in the evening, build a fire, hang out. Or we did."

"Who drove, besides you?"

"Pat, Susan, and Philip came together, I think, and Billy and Mike were in Mike's truck. They already had the fire going when I got there. I stopped off for Roslyn, but she didn't want to go."

"Why?"

"She doesn't much drink."

"Could you point out the farm pond on google maps?" KD handed him her phone with the app open on their current location.

Jimmy scrolled northwest on the map and then magnified the area by a county road. "Right there. Blow up the map enough and you can see the pond."

"Thanks." KD took her phone back. "Can you think of any place they might have gone after they left the pond?"

"It was late. Everyone had work the next day. I don't know anything that happened after I left. I went home and went to bed."

"Anything else you can think of?"

"Are you really planning on solving this case, or are you just doing a walk-through so you can go home?"

KD studied his face. "We're going to do our best." She handed him her card. "Give me a call if you think of anything else."

Jimmy Crowder watched them walk back down the sidewalk to their car. They weren't being paid to look the other way. Maybe they'd find out something. Maybe they'd get justice for Pat and Susan, Billy, Mike, and Philip. At least find the guys who did the killing.

The front door opened, and Roslyn's mom stepped out onto the porch. She was still dressed in slacks and a sweater from her office manager job. "I didn't realize you were out here. Who were those people?"

"Federal investigators looking into the murders."

"I thought your dad was handling it."

"He is. They just want to make sure it's not a terrorism case."

"Terrorism? In Mercy Creek? Seems farfetched to me."

3

KD and Blunt climbed into their rented Camry. "That kid was really busted up," Blunt said.

"Yeah, but was it all grief or was part of it guilt?"

"Guilt for still being alive?"

"Or guilt from knowing what really happened."

"You think he set his friends up?"

"No, but he's the only one alive. He's got to know more than he told us."

KD pulled away from the Billings house and drove out to Payne's farm pond, which was down a rutted dirt driveway off a county road. In the distance on the other side of the pond was an old, two-story farmhouse. A small dock slanted into the pond at the end of the driveway. A picnic table sat under a grove of maple trees on the right. On the other side of the turnaround on the left, a steel firepit sat out in the open, a stack of firewood nearby under a weathered brown tarp.

KD turned the Camry around, pointing back down the driveway, before she and Blunt got out and walked over to the firepit.

"No police tape," Blunt said.

"Sheriff said they didn't find anything out here."

"So this is where they were at," Blunt said. "Six people and three vehicles. Eleven-thirty at night. Having a little party."

"Crowder left with Mateo Smits. His car was driven home by another guy."

"That leaves five people and two vehicles."

"Ground's trampled, grass is worn down as you would expect, but there's nothing to indicate a fight," KD said. "Just good wholesome country fun."

"So at least—what? Three men with guns?"

"If they took them from here, at least four, if they all came in one vehicle. Two to drive off Pat's and Mike's trucks, two to control the four men and one woman. If it was four, they tied them up and loaded them into something big, a van or a Suburban—something like that, I'd guess."

"And they took them away to a place they could control."

"Their vehicles disappeared into a chop shop somewhere."

"And Jimmy Crowder was exempted. Why?" Blunt asked.

"His dad's the sheriff?"

"Maybe he's dirty. Maybe his dad is dirty. Maybe the drug cartel knew they didn't have to worry about him."

"Maybe he just got lucky. Maybe R&G isn't a cartel front. Maybe R&G is legit and just infiltrated with cartel members and bought-off drivers." KD looked off across the farm field. "Middle of nowhere. No risk of being spied on here. They just rolled up, took them, and drove away. Where to?"

Blunt kicked at the loose dirt. "Or they just dealt with them here."

"Sheriff said they searched."

"How carefully? A rake and a couple of buckets of water would clear away any visible evidence." He picked up a stick, went to the firepit, and stirred through the ashes. "This fire is burned completely down to white ash. No unburned ends, no half-burned fragments."

"Meaning?"

"I don't know. Just doesn't seem normal." He arced the stick into the pond. "And God knows what's at the bottom of the pond. We done here?"

"Yeah, let's go get some supper."

THE NEXT MORNING, KD and Blunt received an encrypted email from Tina Han at the NDA offices. She'd gotten a look at an ATF meta-analysis that indicated that hundreds of semiautomatic rifles and handguns purchased across the upper Midwest over the last year were unaccounted for.

"We already knew that guns were moving south," Blunt said.

"But this analysis means it's a lot more than just a pallet or two hidden on a few trucks," KD said. "This is a large-scale, ongoing enterprise. Where does the money come from? To buy this number of guns, you've got to be selling a lot of drugs."

"So there ought to be more arrests and seizures than we're seeing."

"Exactly. Unless this operation is protected."

After breakfast, KD and Blunt drove around Mercy Creek, Blunt behind the wheel, KD working down a list of the houses that belonged to city and county officials. The county commissioners, the sheriff, the mayor, the city council members, even the county court clerk and the county judge, all seemed to have nicer homes and nicer cars than you would expect for their salaries.

"On the surface," Blunt said, "it looks like the corruption here extends throughout the city and county government."

"But what are they being asked to do? Twenty or thirty thousand a year goes a long way around here. Are they being asked to turn a blind eye or are they engaging in active crime?"

"What's the profile here? R&G came in after the plastic bottle plant and the vinyl siding plant folded up during the recession. But this is the county seat. County government jobs, law offices, banks. Walmart and HyVee grocery."

"The downtown is weak, but I bet it's been that way since the mall opened up out at the freeway," KD replied.

"And now the mall is weak because all the smaller malls are weak."

"So R&G is one of the few major private sector employers."

"That's warehouse work and truck driving. Some people getting hired to work construction out-of-town."

"But that's Fords and starter homes, not Caddies and McMansions. Let's have Tina dig into R&G, the county officials, and the dead kids. We need to know who's spending money they shouldn't have."

MEANWHILE, Henry Granger sat in his Escalade in the parking lot at the R&G warehouse facility. Yesterday, the NDA investigators had talked with the dead kids' parents, Mateo, and Jimmy, and they'd gone out to the farm pond. What were they up to? Granger called the sheriff on a burner phone. "Why are the NDA investigators still here? It's been three days."

"They aren't sharing anything with me."

"They were talking with Jimmy on his girlfriend's front porch yesterday."

"Of course they're talking to him. He was best friends with everyone who was killed."

"He better keep quiet."

"What can he tell them? He doesn't know anything about what happened, does he? And he gives Mateo an alibi."

"What makes you think Mateo needs an alibi?"

"Nothing. I'm just saying he has one."

"You need to get rid of those investigators."

"How do I do that? I don't have any jurisdiction over them. If I put pressure on them, all it's going to do is make them suspicious."

"I'm going to put Jimmy back to work."

"Do you think he's ready?"

"Stewing all day isn't helping him. He needs something else on his mind."

"He's grieving. Give him a few more days."

"Okay. Two more days, but then he goes back in the mix. Keep him away from those investigators."

. . .

THE NEXT AFTERNOON, KD and Blunt got a call from Tina Han. "R&G has two big projects going right now. A strip mall in Eagle Grove, Oklahoma, and an elementary school in Comanche Pass, Texas. Everything I've been able to find out thus far seem entirely legit. They've had jobs up and down I-35 for the last few years. They have centralized warehouses where they store the materials and then move them on site as needed."

"Thanks, Tina. You have anything on the county employees and the dead kids?"

"It'll take a few more days."

KD pulled up google maps on her phone. "Two projects on Interstate 35. The Texas one is south of San Antonio—easy striking distance of the US border at Laredo."

"So the FBI, the ATF, and the DEA have been coordinating on a corruption probe," Blunt said. "An FBI undercover fingers an R&G semitruck. Then he's killed, along with four locals, after the truck is busted. Looks like there's too much money in Mercy Creek and not enough drug enforcement. Is it coincidence, or is R&G Construction running a drug and gun pipeline, moving drugs up into the Midwest and guns down into Mexico?"

"That's a theory, but how much driving does R&G actually do up and down the I-35 corridor?"

"I bet Jimmy Crowder could tell us."

They drove downtown, where they spotted Jimmy's truck parked on the street in front of Scooter's Games. Inside, several young men were playing pinball at the machines near the front door. Two couples were playing pool at the front pool table, and Jimmy was shooting pool by himself at the back table. He was racking the balls as they walked up to him.

"Jimmy," KD said, "You always shoot pool by yourself?"

He set the balls and lifted the rack. "I do now. Roslyn's off with her mom."

"This something you used to do with the gang?"

"Most Tuesdays."

"We've been looking for you. Can we ask you a few more questions?

"Shoot."

"You do a lot of long-distance driving for R&G?"

"Sure. R&G has big projects going on down in Oklahoma and Texas. Truckloads of materials get shipped in from Chicago. We distribute them down to the construction sites and bring back unused material. I'm on the road all week half the time. Overtime is great."

"What about Pat?"

"Oh, yeah. We'd hang out together at night if we were long-hauling down to Texas, waiting on a return load."

"What do you carry in a return load?"

"Materials that weren't needed, materials sent by mistake—happens more that you'd think. Actual inventory doesn't always match what the computer says. What's this got to do with the murders?"

"Probably nothing. Just trying to put together a complete picture."

"Anything else?"

"Not right now. Thanks for your cooperation."

KD and Blunt went back out to their car.

"So R&G trucks are going south and back up north all the time," KD said.

"Perfect cover for moving drugs or guns."

"But is R&G a front for a drug cartel, or has it just been infiltrated by gangsters piggybacking on its legitimate loads? We don't have enough info to know yet."

"It's just a matter of scale."

"But the larger the scale, the more likely there's ongoing corruption of cops and public officials."

AFTER KD and Blunt went into Scooter's Games, the man who was tailing them called Smits, who called Granger at home. "The NDA investigators are talking to Jimmy again."

"Where at?"

"Scooter's."

"I told the sheriff to keep his son on a short leash."

"Well, that's not working."

The line was quiet for a moment.

"Henry?"

"Time to try something different. Mr. Juarez wants everything kept quiet, but that's not working. I want to know how these investigators will react if we push them a little bit."

"Something physical?"

"No, not yet. Just a sign to let them know that we can do whatever we want."

"Won't that make them more suspicious?"

"They're already suspicious or they would have left town."

"I'll take care of it."

Granger ended the call and called the sheriff. "Your son's talking with the investigators again."

"Damn it."

"Do you have control of him or not?"

"I'll make myself clear."

"You do that."

AN HOUR LATER, when Jimmy came out of Scooter's Games carrying his pool cue, he spotted his father's Explorer parked across the street and crossed over to it. The sheriff lowered his window.

"You looking for me?" Jimmy said.

"Get in."

Jimmy got in the passenger's side.

"You need to stay away from Thorne and Blunt."

"I wasn't looking for them. I was just shooting some pool."

"Doesn't matter. Stop answering their questions."

"Why? I want the murderers to pay. And Thorne and Blunt are the only ones looking for them."

"Put your big boy pants on. We both know who killed your friends, and we both know why."

"They weren't narcs."

"Something was bound to happen after that semi of guns was intercepted. If it wasn't one of your friends, why did Thorne and Blunt show up? Investigating terrorists, my ass."

"I'm only going to help them find the killers, not tell about anything else. Granger could give the killers up if he wanted to."

"He's not going to do that. He ordered your friends killed. Made sure nothing would happen to you."

"But they were innocent. There has to be some accountability. Someone has got to pay for killing them."

"And I'm looking for the killers. If I find them, I'll make Henry give them up. But you need to quit talking to Thorne and Blunt."

THE NEXT MORNING, when KD and Blunt came out into the Holiday Inn Express parking lot, the right front tire on the Camry was flat. Blunt squatted down to examine it.

"What do you think?" KD asked.

"Bet it turns out to be a puncture."

KD got the temporary spare out of the trunk. Blunt loosened the lug nuts on the flat tire before he jacked it up. He pulled off the wheel. KD rolled him the spare.

"Guest we're pissing somebody off," Blunt said.

"So we must be on the right track," KD replied.

Blunt pushed the temporary spare into place and started putting on the lug nuts.

"You know," KD said, "thinking about this case, my mind keeps coming back to Susan. There's something about her I'm not understanding."

"Like why she's the only woman in this group of friends?"

"Exactly. If there's anything going on there that we need to know about."

KD heaved the flat tire into the trunk. Blunt tossed the jack down beside it. "That's something to ask Jimmy Crowder, I guess."

They headed down Johnson Boulevard toward town, KD driving. "Let's drop off the tire to be fixed and go get breakfast."

Blunt googled up a tire store. "Gregson's Firestone is on the way to Poppa Joe's."

"The diner downtown? Don't you want to try someplace new?"

"Not for breakfast. It's Jimmy Crowder's go-to place." Blunt looked over his shoulder. "That utility van is awful close."

"I know. I can't go any faster on this temporary spare."

Two cars flew by, headed in the other direction. Then the van shot past them, swung in tight in front of them, and braked hard. KD stomped on her brakes and swung onto the shoulder. The van shot forward and disappeared down the road. "Asshole."

"Nice driving."

"Did you get the license plate?"

"Covered in mud."

"That guy just a jerk or did he come with the flat tire?"

"Who knows?"

They dropped the flat tire off to be fixed and then parked in a metered spot down the street from Poppa Joe's Diner. Inside, all the booths were full, but Jimmy Crowder was in there, sitting in a booth by himself. KD and Blunt slid in opposite him. "Mind if we join you?"

"No, I guess not. I just ordered." He waived for the waitress to come back. She looked at him expectantly. "Cindy, can we get two menus?"

"Sure, hon." She turned to KD and Blunt. "You want coffee?"

"Please," they both said.

"Lucky we spotted you," KD said. "Might have been a wait."

"It's prime time right now."

"Can I ask a few more questions?"

"I guess."

"Something I've been wondering about. You guys and Susan. She was always part of the group?"

"From kindergarten. She was a tomboy in grade school. By the time she quit fighting and climbing, she was just another one of us."

"But she was Pat's girl?"

"I don't want you to get the wrong impression, but Susan had a mind of her own. Better not get too attached to her, if you get my drift."

"Was she cheating on Pat?"

"The way she would put it, it's only cheating if you promised not to."

"So who was the other guy?"

"Philip. I'm pretty sure they were sneaking around on the side."

"Had any of the others of you dated her?"

"I did in high school. Before Roslyn. But it became clear—look, Susan was one of my best friends, but we had different ideas about monogamy."

"Her mom thinks Pat should have married her."

"I think he would have, but I don't think she wanted to get married."

The waitress brought their coffee. "Ready to order?"

KD and Blunt both ordered the breakfast special—two eggs, bacon, and wheat toast. Blunt put sugar and creamer in his coffee. "Sorry we keep having questions."

"No problem," Jimmy said. "Anything I can do."

"You seeing a therapist?" KD asked.

"I'm doing okay."

"It's pretty tough—what you've been through."

"I'm kind of down, but it's one day at a time."

"When you going back to work?" Blunt asked.

"Tomorrow. It's about time. Need something to fill my day."

Jimmy's food came first. He was dabbing the last of his egg yolk with the last corner of toast when the waitress came by with KD's and Blunt's plates. "Cindy, can I get my check?"

"Sure, hon."

"We'll take care of it," KD said.

"You sure?"

"Absolutely."

"Thanks."

The waitress nodded. "More coffee?"

"Yes," Blunt said.

"I'm fine," KD said.

Jimmy scooted out of the booth and headed for the door. The waitress warmed up Blunt's coffee and took Jimmy's plate.

"So," Blunt said, "Large amounts of guns in the upper Midwest are unaccounted for. R&G has major projects in Oklahoma and Texas. Pat is driving materials down from the warehouse. Susan is sleeping with Pat and Philip. One shipment of guns was intercepted. Those are our facts."

KD nodded. "So what does Pat know? Is he muling guns south to Mexico and drugs up into the Midwest? Is he talking to Susan, and Susan talking to Philip? Was she Philip's source? Is that why they were all killed?"

"And Jimmy recommended Pat for the job."

"So is Jimmy in on the smuggling, or did Pat get started on that on his own?"

"Jimmy goes back to work tomorrow," Blunt said. "We need to get a look at his tractor-trailer rig before he leaves."

"I'll call Tina to get the license plate numbers of his semitruck."

MIDMORNING, the two men following KD and Blunt reported in to Smits that they had seen them eating breakfast with Jimmy Crowder. After lunch, Smits met with Henry Granger in his office at the R&G warehouses.

"Well?" Granger asked.

Smits sat down in the low-back chair facing Granger's desk. "They went straight from the flat tire and the side swipe to hunting down Jimmy."

"So that's the third time these assholes have met with him," Granger said.

"That we know of."

"Are you telling me your guys don't know what they're doing?"

"No, Henry, I'm just saying we only know what we know."

"Well, Jimmy's driving tomorrow, so he won't be available to answer any more questions."

"Where are you sending him?"

"First to Eagle Grove, then on to Comanche Pass, where we'll make him wait for a return load. That way, he'll be out of the way while we work on these NDA assholes. They don't want to take a hint, so it's time to step up our game. Find a way to grab one of them, apply some pressure, see if we can find out why they're still snooping around."

"Gotcha. Any restrictions?"

"Don't kill them. That's still a step too far. We don't want to attract Mr. Juarez's attention or more Feds. Find out what they know. Convince them they should leave."

LATER, while Granger was driving home from work, after he turned into the neighborhood of two-story brick houses where he lived, he got a call on his burner from Mr. Juarez. He pulled over on the side of the street two blocks from his house to take the call. "Mr. Juarez."

"Henry. I hear from my contacts that the NDA investigators are still in Mercy Creek."

"Nothing to worry about."

"Don't underestimate them. I've seen their job files. They're both skilled military operators with covert ops experience."

"There's nothing for them to find. We're keeping a low profile, just like you asked."

"Are you sure everything's under control? My friends tell me that the NDA is not sharing any information about their investigation—not with the FBI, not with the ATF, not with the state police. That, my friend, is worrying."

"The killings were a blunder. I admit it. But all the loose ends have been cleaned up. And we haven't lost a shipment since that one load of guns. They aren't sharing anything because they don't have anything to share."

"Then let's make sure it stays that way." Mr. Juarez ended the call.

Granger pulled away from the curb. Skilled operators? He needed to get Mr. Juarez off his back. Picking up one of the investigators, sweating them—that was the right call. That was the only way to find out what they knew. And then he'd know what he needed to do to convince them to leave, and everything would go back to normal.

LATE THAT NIGHT, KD and Blunt, wearing dark clothes, parked on Davis Street a block away from the R&G warehouse complex and walked up the alley between A-1 Home Heating and Cooling company and City Recycling Center to reach the chain-link fence surrounding the R&G facility. There were no surveillance cameras in sight, and the only outdoor lights were positioned at the front gate and over the door to the company offices, which were located in the nearest warehouse. Two semitrucks sat in the parking lot to the left of the warehouse. KD reached into her backpack, took out a set of night vision binoculars, and examined the license plates attached to the fronts of the trucks. The semitruck closest to the warehouse, a cab attached to a tarp-covered flat load trailer, bore Jimmy Crowder's license plate. "We're in business," she whispered.

They climbed the fence, dropped down inside the compound, and scurried across the open parking lot. Vehicle noises echoed through the nearby buildings from the freeway in the distance. When they reached the semitrucks, they slipped in between the wall of the warehouse and Jimmy Crowder's semitruck.

"You're on," KD said.

KD positioned herself by the front wheel of the truck cab. Blunt crept to the back of the trailer, unhooked two bungee cords on the tarp covering the load, crawled under the tarp, and turned on his penlight. Drywall, steel two-by-fours, bags of drywall compound, boxes of drywall screws. The tarp was on too tight for him to crawl up through the materials. He backed out onto the ground and rehooked the bungee cords.

KD glanced back at him. He shook his head. He went about

halfway up on the left side of the trailer and repeated the process. Nothing.

As he dropped back down to the ground, KD put her hand on his shoulder. "Two guys," she whispered. "At eleven o'clock, coming from the front of the warehouse."

They squatted below the trailer. Two men, blue uniforms and caps, sidearms in holsters, were walking across the front of the parking lot. Blunt glanced at KD. She pointed toward the front of the rig. They slipped behind the nearest wheel. The security guards walked along, chatting, until they reached the fence, where they followed along the perimeter of the property until they disappeared around the back of the warehouse.

KD nodded.

Blunt unhooked two bungee cords near the front left of the trailer and wriggled under the tarp, his penlight in his mouth. This time he crouched up on all fours, pushing his back into the tarp. A long, rectangular box was packed between two boxes labeled *foundation coating*. He crawled forward, cut the tape on the box with his pocketknife, and shined his penlight inside. Semiautomatic rifles wrapped in newspaper. He slipped back out and rehooked the bungee cords.

"Found them," he whispered.

KD reached into her backpack, pulled out a GPS tracker, and attached it to the underside of the trailer. Then they ran back to the fence, keeping an eye out for the guards, and climbed over.

"How many guns were there?" KD asked.

"I don't know. I looked in one box, saw assault-type rifles, that's all."

When they got back to the Camry, KD called Tina and reached her voice mail. "I activated a GPS tracker. It should start moving early tomorrow morning."

THE NEXT MORNING, Jimmy Crowder pulled out of the R&G warehouse parking lot at 5:00 a.m. to make the nine-hour run down to their warehouse in Eagle Grove, Oklahoma. The weather was great for driving once the sun rose, clear but not bright, and he slipped through Kansas City at the end of the morning rush and through Wichita before lunch. He ate in the truck, peed in a milk jug, drove just slowly enough to avoid the state troopers, and pulled into the R&G Eagle Grove warehouse at 2:15 p.m., where he backed his trailer into its designated spot. Then he got out of his cab and went into the office.

Perry, the office manager, spat tobacco juice into a can. "Hey, Jimmy."

"Be right with you."

Jimmy went into the restroom, used the urinal, washed his hands, and rinsed his face with cold water before he came out.

"You made good time," Perry said. "Bet you didn't stop."

"You're right." Jimmy pulled some paperwork out of his back pocket. "Here's the bill of lading."

Perry glance at it and then put it into his inbox. "Girls will check the computer when they get back from break."

"Got one for me to take back?"

"Got one for you going down to Texas. It'll be ready in about four hours. Take the loaner car, go get something to eat."

Jimmy picked up the keys to a beat-up Corolla that R&G kept on site for truckdrivers to borrow and started across the parking lot. He glanced at his watch. Roslyn would be in her office now. He got out his phone and speed-dialed her. "Hey, babe."

"Hey, Jimmy. This is a nice surprise. What's up?"

"I just got to Eagle Grove. Thought I'd be coming back tonight, but I'm going to Comanche Pass instead. So if somebody slips into your bed in the middle of the night, it's not me."

"Very funny. When will you be back?"

"I'm not sure. Not tomorrow or the next day. It'll be in the morning when I get there, I'll need a night's sleep, and they won't send me north without a load."

"My mom's expecting you for dinner on Saturday."

"I'll do the best I can. Listen, I've got to go."

"I love you."

"I love you, too."

MEANWHILE, KD and Blunt were driving down Elm Street, KD behind the wheel, when Blunt got a call from Tina Han. He put it on speaker. "Your truck is parked at the R&G warehouse in Eagle Grove, Oklahoma."

"Thanks, Tina. Let us know if it starts moving again."

"Will do. I've also got the financial info on the county employees and the dead kids."

"Give us the highlights."

"County officials do own more property than they should, but not that much more. The dead kids are exactly as advertised, except for Pat Green."

"How much?"

"Twenty thousand in savings."

"He'd have to be living off his parents to save that much."

"What about the Crowders?"

"The sheriff is squeaky clean, and the son has exactly what you'd expect a truckdriver to have if he was living at home and saving up for a house down payment. I'll email the report when I get off the phone."

"Thanks, Tina."

Blunt ended the call. He glanced at KD. "So Pat Green was probably muling drugs and guns, and the county officials are probably better than he was at covering up their graft."

"But how far does this conspiracy go? We need to chase those guns," KD said.

"Think they'll be there by the time we can get there?"

"They're our best lead."

KD pulled into the Casey's General Store on the corner.

Blunt opened the map app on his phone. "It's a nine-hour drive."

KD tapped on the map app on her phone. "But it's an hour to the Des Moines airport. A four-hour flight down to Oklahoma City.

Another hour, hour and a half to Eagle Grove. If you make the 3:30 flight, you could be there by 10:00 p.m."

"Guns will probably be gone."

"But you'll still have a chance to recon that warehouse."

"Okay. Let me know if you hear from Tina. Guess I need a car." Blunt tapped on his map app. "Only rental place in town is the Enterprise out near the freeway."

KD made a U-turn around the gas pumps in front of the Casey's General Store and turned right, heading toward the freeway. "While you're getting the car, I'll get the plane tickets, forward them to your email."

"Hope it's worth the trouble."

"We've got to start somewhere."

BLUNT DROVE east on the beltway around Eagle Grove, Oklahoma, to the industrial area next to the freeway. He parked on the street next to a cardboard box manufacturing plant two blocks west of the R&G warehouse facilities. He was dressed in a dark jacket and dark pants, a small black bookbag over his shoulder. He made his way along the deserted streets, acting as if he was in no particular hurry, until he came to R&G's chain-link fence. The R&G warehouse facilities here were built on the same template as the Mercy Creek facilities— parking lot for tractor-trailer rigs and buildings for storing materials, one of which contained the offices, only there were two building here, not three. Two uniformed security guards came from the far side of the second warehouse, walked across the front of the parking lot, and went into the offices.

Blunt checked the GPS app on his phone. The trailer he was looking for was still there, one of three fully loaded trailers parked beside the nearest warehouse. He glanced up and down. No one in sight. He climbed the fence, dropped down onto the asphalt, and scurried across the open parking lot until he reached the cover of the first trailer.

He looked at his GPS app. The second trailer was the one he was looking for. He went around to the front right side and felt under the trailer beside the wheel for the GPS tracker. There it was. He unhooked two bungee cords, crawled under the tarp, and turned on his penlight. The box containing the rifles was gone. And the other boxes were different from the ones he'd seen before. The trailer had been reloaded. He turned off his penlight and backed out. Just as he put his feet on the ground, a semitruck sounded its horn. He looked toward the gate. The semitruck pulled up, the gate opened, and the truck rolled into the parking lot. He crouched under the trailer, hidden by a wheel, and waited.

The truck stopped in the open, near the office door. The driver climbed out and went into the building. Blunt slipped along the side of the warehouse and around the back corner. He shined his penlight through the windows, keeping the beam angled down. All he saw were stacks of boxes, and pallets of cut lumber, plywood, and other building materials. He ran across the open area to the next ware-house. More of the same.

Shouting and truck noises came from the front parking lot. Blunt snuck back to the corner of the first warehouse, where he could see what was going on. The truck that had just arrived had dropped its original trailer and was now backing up to the trailer with the GPS tracker on it. Two men on the ground checked the trailer height, motioned the truck cab back, and locked the king pin on the trailer into place after the cab connected with the trailer. Then they connected the electrical and air cables, and waved up at the driver and yelled something. The driver waved back and drove away with the trailer with the tracker on it.

Blunt waited for the men to go back into the office before he ran across the parking lot and climbed over the fence. As he walked down the street to his car, he called KD to fill her in. "Guns were gone. Trailer had been reloaded. It's on the move."

"Maybe it will go someplace interesting."

"I guess we'll find out. I'll head back to Oklahoma City and catch a morning flight, so I'll be in Mercy Creek in the afternoon."

"See you then."

4

The next morning, while KD was still at breakfast in the diner across the highway from the Holiday Inn Express, she got a call from Tina. "The tracker is back at the R&G warehouse in Mercy Creek."

"Thanks."

That was quick. The driver must have driven straight back from Eagle Grove. Wonder what he was carrying? She finished her eggs and took her last gulp of coffee. Maybe she should roll around to R&G just to see what she could see. She left a tip on the table, paid at the cash register, and walked out to her car.

KD parked on the other side of the R&G warehouses, on the shoulder of a county road beside a cornfield. Combines were moving across the field in the distance, trucks following to collect the corn. She got out a set of binoculars and scanned the warehouse complex through the chain-link fence. Only one trailer was being unloaded. She guessed it was the trailer with the tracker on it.

She got out of her car and walked up to the fence, but it didn't improve her view. She wasn't going to find out much from surveillance. She still thought Jimmy Crowder knew more than he was sharing. They needed to find a way to get him to open up. Either him or someone else. She crossed the road, sat back down in the driver's seat, tossed the binoculars into the passenger seat.

Before she could start the car, she felt the end of a gun barrel pressed against her neck.

"Keep your hands on the steering wheel," the voice behind her said. "You can die or not die. It's up to you."

Two men wearing ski masks ran up out of the corn. One opened her car door, the other grabbed her by the collar of her shirt, threw her down on the gravel, and put his knee in her back. The first guy pulled the SIG Sauer from her hip and then zip-tied her wrists behind her back. The second guy put a bag on her head. They heaved her up by the arms, dragged her into the back floorboard and sat in the back seat with their feet on top of her.

"Drive," one of them said.

The Camry bounced down the county road. KD willed herself into survival mode, controlling her heart rate. Stupid mistake. Getting scooped up like an amateur. Still, if they wanted to kill her, she'd already be dead. So they wanted something, which meant she had time. She needed information and opportunity if she were going to escape. She kept quiet, hoping to hear something that would tell her who these guys were or where they were taking her, but all she heard was breathing and indistinct road noise. When they finally stopped, they dragged her out of the floorboard onto hardpacked dirt, pulled her to her feet, and rushed her through a creaking door into a building where they pushed her down into a wooden chair and zip-tied her arms to the arms and her legs to the legs.

She tried to see through the bag, but all she could make out were gray shapes. "Why am I here?"

"To do whatever we want, Missy. You don't mind your business; we don't mind ours."

Another voice cut in. "Maybe we take your pants, stake you out, let the dogs have you."

"Afterward," a third voice said. "We're not in a hurry."

Bluster. Used to dealing with civilians. KD slowed her breathing, listening, trying to tell as much as she could from the sounds. Bird song in the distance. Faint smell of manure. But no dogs. At least not now. She had three kidnappers to content with. As long as she was zip-tied to the chair, there was nothing she could do. They could beat her unconscious and rape her. Their only limits were their orders and their discipline in following their orders.

"Where's your black lover?" It was the second voice. KD didn't reply. Someone kicked the chair.

"Your partner," the first voice said, "where is he?"

She didn't reply.

"She must be too thirsty to talk," the third voice said.

She heard scraping. Ice water poured down on her head, ice cubes cascading down her body, the freezing water soaking her clothes. The wet bag clung to her face, choking her. She opened her mouth wide, trying to suck in air, struggling against the zip-ties. Something large banged against her side, knocking the chair over. Her shoulder hit the ground hard. Her head bounced. But the bag was still plastered to her face, and she was still choking.

"Hold still," the first voice said.

She felt the sole of a boot on her head, holding it in place, and then the rush of fresh air. He'd cut a mouth hole. The chair was righted. She breathed deep, trying to avoid hyperventilating.

Someone smacked her face. "Wake up," the third voice said. "Why did you come here?"

"You're going to answer our questions," the first voice said. "Easy or hard, it's up to you."

So they can beat me, but they probably can't kill me, at least not right now, she thought. I may have to tell them something eventually, but if I hold on long enough, it won't have to be the truth.

Someone punched her in the face. "What are you doing in Mercy Creek?"

SHORTLY AFTER 3:00 P.M., Blunt took the freeway exit into Mercy Creek, and drove down Johnson Boulevard, headed toward the Enterprise Rent-A-Car to drop off his car. He put his phone on speaker and speed-dialed KD, but the call immediately rolled over to voice mail. He pulled into the mall parking lot, parked in front of the main entrance, and tried again. Voice mail. Where was she?

He drove back toward the freeway and pulled into the Holiday Inn Express. Their car wasn't there. Still, he went upstairs and knocked on her door. No answer. He went down to the front desk. The day receptionist—a middle-age, blonde woman worrying a piece of chewing gum while she studied the computer—was still there.

"Have you seen my partner?"

"Not since early this morning."

"Tall, dark brown hair—"

"I know what she looks like, hon. She left out early. Hasn't been back, or at least she didn't walk through the lobby."

"Thanks."

Blunt drove downtown, circled by the Billings house, the county jail, Poppa Joe's, and then drove out to the R&G warehouses, but KD's car was nowhere. He tried her phone again, but it went straight to voice mail. Must be turned off. He called Tina.

"Can you track KD's phone?"

"Hang on," she replied. In a few moments, she came back on. "No. The phone's dead. What's up?"

"I'll get back to you."

He called the sheriff.

"Sheriff Crowder? This is Agent Blunt."

"What can I do for you?"

"Agent Thorne is missing."

"How so?"

"She's not answering her phone. She's not at the Holiday Inn. I haven't been able to find her around town."

"I thought you two always went around together."

"I had to go out of town."

"When did you speak to her last?"

"Last night."

"When did you get back in town?"

"Around three o'clock."

"You didn't call her earlier today?"

"No."

"So you've been looking about an hour. That doesn't sound like an emergency to me. Her phone's turned off. Maybe she's interviewing somebody, doesn't want to be interrupted."

Blunt drove back out to the mall, circled the parking lot, but KD's Camry wasn't there. Then he drove over to the Walmart. There it was, hiding between two pickup trucks around the side of the building. He parked in the nearest empty spot, went into the Walmart, looked up and down the aisles and in the seating at the coffee shop. He called the sheriff back.

"I found her car."

"Where?"

"North side of the Walmart."

"You look in the store?"

"She's not here."

"Okay, now you've got my interest. I'm on my way."

Blunt was leaning against the trunk of his car when the sheriff drove around the side of the Walmart, parked in the lane behind KD's Camry, and got out.

He nodded at Blunt and then gestured toward KD's car. "This the car?"

"Yeah."

"Probably a wild goose chase." He walked around the Camry. "Mud and pea gravel in the tire tread. You been out in the country?"

"Second day we were here, we went out to Payne's farm pond."

"No pea gravel out there. Anywhere else?"

"That's it."

The sheriff stood looking at the rental car with his hand on his face. If anything happened to Thorne, the county would be crawling with Feds. Henry couldn't be that stupid. What was his game?

Blunt folded his arms across his chest. "So, do you think it's time to do something?"

"I still don't think there's anything to worry about, but let's start a search just to be on the safe side."

. . .

WHEN KD WOKE UP, her clothes were still wet, but the room was dark. What time was it? She'd felt worse, but not in a long time. The insects were loud. It must be dusk or later. She twisted from side to side, testing the chair, and no one spoke or kicked or punched. They must have gone to dinner. Or maybe they'd reported in and were awaiting orders.

She twisted the chair back and forth. The joints from the arms to the back were loose, but more on the left than the right. She tried to hop, kicking her legs forward as she bounced back. She felt a side rail fall from the back right leg. She hopped up on her feet and hopped back. The right back leg gave way and she crashed onto the ground. She saw stars, shook her head, tried to move her arms. The right chair arm had broken loose. She fished the chair arm through the zip tie to get her arm free. She pulled the bag off her head. A few minutes later, she was free.

Moonlight came in through windows on the right. She was in a barn. A big water cooler lay on its side nearby, its lid on the other side of her broken-up chair. How long had she been here? She glanced around. No gun, no knife, no shovel, no water. They hadn't really asked her anything. Didn't know how to ask. She peeked out the door. No vehicles out front. So what was the point? She stumbled out into the yard and started toward the road, weaving like a drunk. Get a grip. Save your life.

She was moving with more confidence by the time she got to the road. If they were hoping to scare her, they'd made a mistake. They'd simply taught her to be more careful. She jogged down the shoulder of the road. Which way back to town? She saw headlights come up from behind her. She ran down into the right-of-way ditch. Then she heard the familiar siren tap of a police cruiser. It was worth the chance. She climbed out of the ditch and waived her arms. The sheriff's Ford Explorer stopped in the road, its headlights illuminating her. The sheriff got out.

"We've been looking everywhere for you. Get in the truck." He took her by the arm and led her into the passenger seat.

"You got any water?"

He turned on the inside lights and fished a bottle of water out of the back seat floorboard.

She drank it down.

"You look like hell."

"I was being held in a barn back up the road there."

The sheriff got on his radio. "Send two cars out to the barn at the abandoned Milo place on Fish Trap Road. I want it taped off and processed."

KD leaned back in her seat, the empty water bottle between her thighs.

"That eye doesn't look so good. I'm taking you to the hospital."

"How long have you been looking?"

"Since four-thirty or so. Blunt couldn't reach you by phone. Then we found your rental car parked at the Walmart."

The sheriff turned off the interior lights and put the Explorer in drive. "Put your seat belt on."

BLUNT FOUND KD sitting on the side of a bed in a bay in the emergency department, trying to button the shirt the nurse found for her in the lost and found. Her right eye was taped, and she had a deep bruise running down her left cheek.

"Hey," he said.

"Hey yourself."

"You look like shit."

"Thanks."

"How did they manage to not break your nose?"

"Always the comedian."

"Doctors letting you leave here?"

"They sure as hell don't want me to stay."

A nurse stepped into the bay carrying a clipboard. "Visitors aren't allowed back here."

Blunt smiled. "I'm her next of kin."

She rolled her eyes and turned to KD. "You sure you're ready to leave, Ms. Thorne?"

"Absolutely."

"Let me help you with that." She finished buttoning KD's shirt. "You have to take it easy."

"I promise."

"So, for the record, you declined the rape kit, and you want to be released."

"Yes."

"Sign the bottom of the form."

KD signed. The nurse turned to Blunt. "She's all yours."

Blunt picked up the bag that contained KD's dirty clothes. "Left or right, Doc?"

"Left."

Blunt moved to her left side and helped her onto her feet. "You'll be okay tomorrow."

"Yep."

She clung to his right side. He put his arm around her back and under her right arm. "Always feels the worst when there's nothing else to worry about."

When he got her out to his car and into the passenger seat, he said, "So what happened?"

"They beat the hell out of me."

"Nothing else?"

"No. The nurse was being dramatic."

"What did the sheriff say?"

"He asked me questions, I gave him answers."

He put the car in gear. "So the trailer came back?"

"Straight back. But I didn't get a chance to look in it."

"Did you see any of them? The guys who grabbed you?"

"No. They wore masks when they grabbed me, and then they put a bag over my head. Took me to the barn. Threatened me and beat me. And then they left me."

"You sure they weren't coming back?"

"I don't think they were supposed to kill me, just scare me."

"You scared?"

"Yeah, Blunt. I'm scared I'm going to kill them first chance I get."

Blunt smiled. "Can you eat?"

"I'm starving."

"I'll pull through a drive-through along the way."

THE SHERIFF and Henry Granger sat in the sheriff's Ford Explorer in the back corner of the parking lot behind the Salvation Army store downtown. The sheriff watched a homeless man carrying a plastic trash bag stumble down the sidewalk. "You should have told me that you were going to snatch one of the NDA agents."

"Why?" Granger replied. "Were you going to help? You had your chance to warn them off."

"You think they'll leave now? You're just stirring up trouble."

"Maybe. Or maybe she'll think about that beating when she's deciding how hard to push."

"That's just foolishness."

"Look, I'm not going to kill them if I don't have to. Killing the snitch caused enough trouble. But I won't put up with too much interference. Money has got to be made. Everyone's got their hand out."

"Maybe you need to ease up for a little while, that's all I'm saying."

"I'll worry about the NDA agents. You worry about your son. He's bringing a big load back from Texas."

"So soon?"

"Has he got a problem?"

"No."

"So he knows whose side he's on?"

"Yeah."

"Then he needs to focus on his job and quit talking to the investigators."

"He's just easing his mind. He isn't telling them anything."

"He keeps talking to them, eventually he's going to tell them something, whether he intends to or not. You tell him to stay away from them."

"I am telling him."

"Then tell him harder."

THE NEXT MORNING, when KD woke up, it was after 10:00 am. She was still wearing the sweatpants and button-up shirt they'd given her at the hospital. She used the hotel room phone to call Blunt's smart-phone. "Hey, it's me."

"Morning, Doc. How're you feeling?"

"Rode hard, put away wet. Where are you?"

"Out at the barn you were at yesterday. They cleaned it all up after you left."

"Nothing there?"

"Nothing. Want some breakfast?"

"Coffee and whatever you can bring me."

She climbed out of bed and limped into the bathroom, where she stripped off her clothes, and turned on the shower to let it heat up. She looked in the mirror. There were dark boot bruises on her abdomen and thighs, a purple bruise on her shoulder where she'd been hit with something, and face bruises that made her look like she'd lost a prize fight. She lifted the tape under her eye and examined the stitches. Not too bad. Overall, they'd marked her up but hadn't hurt her too much.

She showered, moving slowly and gently. She just finished getting dressed when she heard Blunt's rap on her door.

"You're looking better," he said.

"You're a liar. Where's the coffee?"

He handed her a to-go cup and set a take-out bag on the square table by the window. "Got you a breakfast sandwich."

She sat at the table, sipped her coffee and unwrapped the sandwich.

"Egg and bacon," he continued.

"Thanks, Blunt. What about you?"

"Already ate."

They sat in silence while she ate, him watching her. After she rolled up the wrapper and stuffed it in the bag, she said, "I need a new phone."

Blunt got out his phone, called Tina, and put it on speaker. He and KD took turns explaining what happened. "I'll overnight a new phone, ID, and service weapon. You'll have them tomorrow."

"Thanks," KD said.

"Anything else for us?" Blunt asked.

"Yeah, Eagle Grove has a similar profile to Mercy Creek—lost jobs in the recession, drug problem with very few arrests, the strip mall R&G is building there is a big deal.

"Can you look for other small cities on I-35 that also fit the profile?" KD asked.

"I'm on it."

Blunt ended the call.

KD sipped her coffee. "So the barn was cleaned out?"

"Except for the busted-up chair and the water cooler."

"I wasn't gone from there very long before the sheriff found me, so they must have cleaned up any possible evidence while I was unconscious. I feel like an idiot for getting scooped up." KD set her empty coffee cup on the table. "Let's run through what we know."

"The cartel is moving guns south," Blunt said. "They're using R&G to do it, or they *are* R&G."

"They murdered five people after a load of guns was confiscated, including a guy who worked for them."

"From all appearances, county and city officials are bought off here."

"If Eagle Grove has a similar profile," KD replied, "are the city and county officials bought off there as well?"

"The cartel lost a load of guns, so at least one cop wasn't bought off. What happened to that cop?"

Blunt called Tina again.

"What's up?"

"What happened to the cops that busted the semi of guns?"

"Hold on." They could hear the clicking of her keyboard. "Two sheriff's deputies. One retired and the other changed departments."

"That quickly?"

"Yep. That's what it says."

"Thanks, Tina."

Blunt ended the call.

"Sounds like that bust was a freak accident," KD said.

"Which means the cartel controls at least some of the cops from here down into Oklahoma."

"But how many?"

"Sheriff Crowder must be working with the cartel, or at least looking the other way, but he stopped to help you."

"Because he's not a straight-up crook," KD replied.

"Must be complicated figuring out which parts of his job he's going to do."

"I still think Jimmy Crowder is our best lead around here. He wants to help."

"What makes you say that?"

"He keeps on helping."

"He's gone back to work."

"Wonder if he's in town or on the road."

"You ready for a full day's work, Doc?"

"I can hold my own, Blunt. Let's take back your rental car and see if we can track down Crowder."

GRANGER WAS SITTING at a picnic table in the city park. Three men were sitting across from him, a Latino with a goatee, an older man with a gray ponytail, and a sallow-faced man with missing teeth. Young children, their moms watching over them, were on the swings and monkey bars on the other side of the picnic shelter near the parking lot. Two women were playing pickleball on the tennis court. Granger looked hard at the older guy with a gray ponytail.

"You had her at the barn, and she didn't tell you a thing?"

"We pushed her as hard as we could," the older man replied. "You told us not to kill her. She was unconscious when Mateo called and told us the sheriff was looking for her. We ran out of time."

"But we worked her over good," the Latino said. "She's definitely feeling it today."

"And we cleaned it all up," the man with the missing teeth said. "There was nothing to come back on you."

"You three need to get out of town. Take the load to Chicago. Stay there until I tell you to come back."

"Yes, boss," the older man said.

"Go."

Granger watched them walk away. Was Jimmy still reliable? Maybe he should have died with the others. But then his father would have to go. And killing a sheriff—that would definitely bring state and federal heat. He couldn't have that. He needed peace and quiet to keep the shipments moving. Maybe the NDA agents got the message. Maybe they would decide to move on, or at least stop trying so hard. The sheriff was probably right. They couldn't hang around here forever. God, why couldn't he just catch one break?

5

J immy Crowder drove in the gate at the R&G warehouses in Comanche Pass, Texas, parked in the space next to the office, and went inside. An unshaven man in a wheelchair, checked flannel shirt open over a white T-shirt, sat behind the desk.

"Hey, Jimmy."

"Hey, Rocky."

"It's been a while, hasn't it?"

"Just a month."

"Sorry about Pat. He was a good guy."

"Thanks."

Jimmy handed the truck's bill of lading across the desk. Rocky read over the first page. "Just in time. They need most of these materials at the job site now."

"You got a load for me?"

"About that. It's going to be a few days."

"Come on, man. I don't want to hang around here. My girl's waiting at home."

"Logistics is a bitch." He took a wad of folded twenty dollar bills out of the desk drawer and tossed it to Jimmy. "Get a motel room. Do some gambling, if that's your thing. Just be ready to go when I call."

Jimmy picked up the cash.

"The blue Dodge Dart has the keys in it."

Jimmy put his roller bag into the back seat of the Dodge and drove down the highway to the Double Nickel Casino Resort near the freeway interchange on the other side of Comanche Pass. The parking lot was half empty. He got a room with a balcony overlooking the swimming pool and sat down on the bed. It was going to be a boring few days. Once upon a time, before things were serious with Roslyn, he and Pat would have gone honky-tonking, found some women, made it a real party on the company's dime. But now? Pat was dead. Who the hell got them into that trouble? Mike didn't even take drugs. Billy hadn't sold anything since high school. Philip—what did they really know about him? He always had money, was always ready to party, but he never talked about drugs. Did some sort of IT thing that he worked from home. None of them would have done anything to cross Granger.

Jimmy opened the balcony door and stood on the balcony, watching the families down at the swimming pool. Kids were squealing. Some dad was waving his arms like he was guarding a basketball rim. A mom grabbed a toddler up out of the water and set him on the concrete. Jimmy got out his phone.

"Hey, babe."

"Hey, Jimmy," Roslyn said. "Where are you?"

"I'm stuck down in Comanche Pass. Won't be back for a couple of days."

"That sucks."

"Tell me about it. What're you doing?"

"Going to the movies with the girls."

"What's playing?"

"Some romcom thing Bridget is hot to see. Wish she'd find a boyfriend."

"What happened to the last guy? He didn't last long enough for me to learn his name."

"That's cruel."

"I'm just saying."

"You know Bridget. She's a romantic. She wants a guy to call in the morning, tell her he misses her, you know. Brady was too stoic, I guess."

"Then it's a good thing I called to tell you I'm missing you."

"Is that what you're doing?"

"Yep."

"You going to get up to no good?"

"No, ma'am. Don't do that anymore."

"Listen, honey, I know you're having a hard time."

"I'm okay."

"I'm just saying that if you need to blow off some steam, I wouldn't judge you."

"So it's 'what happens in Comanche Pass, stays in Comanche Pass'?"

"If that's what you need, honey."

"You're the best."

"Took you long enough to notice."

"But I'm not doing anything crazy."

"Okay."

"Enjoy the movie."

"I'll be thinking about you during the kissing parts."

"I love you."

"I love you. Call me tomorrow."

Jimmy ended the call. He needed to go down to one of the restaurants to get something to eat. He changed into his good jeans and a shirt with a collar and went downstairs.

KD AND BLUNT drove around town, looking for Jimmy Crowder at his usual haunts, but he wasn't at Scooter's Games, Ray Bob's Microbrew, or Mercy Creek Park. Out at the movie theater next to the strip mall, KD saw Roslyn come out of the theater with three other women.

"That's Jimmy's girlfriend, isn't it?"

"The blonde?" Blunt replied. "I think you're right."

"Pull over."

KD got out of the car and jogged toward the sidewalk. "Roslyn! Roslyn Billings!"

Roslyn turned from her friends. "Do I know you?"

"I'm KD Thorne."

"Oh, yeah. One of the investigators. Jimmy told me about you. What happened to your face?"

"Long story. I'm looking for Jimmy."

She eyed her suspiciously. "I don't guess I shouldn't say. He's at work."

"At work where?"

"He's down in Comanche Pass, Texas, waiting on a return load." She glanced back toward her friends, who were about to enter an Appleby's. "I've got to go."

"Thanks."

THE NEXT MORNING, KD got the overnight package containing her new SIG Saur, her ID, and her new phone with the address book and apps all set up. Blunt watched her put the ID and phone into her pockets and the pistol into the holster on her hip.

"How you feeling, Doc?"

"I'm a little stiff, but I'm good to go. I've fielded a sixty-pound pack when I was in worse shape than this."

"I hear you."

KD's new smartphone rang. It was Tina. "Comanche Pass also fits the profile. It's a little smaller than Eagle Grove or Mercy Creek, but it's an easy drive to the Mexican border. Major employer is an Indian casino. Of course, that zone is rife with drugs and guns."

"And that's where Jimmy's waiting on a load," KD said.

"I wonder if he'll be carrying more than building materials when he drives north," Blunt said.

"He's staying at the casino hotel," Tina said.

"I guess we better have a look," KD replied.

It was after 7:00 p.m. by the time KD and Blunt rented a car at the Comanche Pass Regional Airport and drove out to the R&G warehouse complex. "It's the same template as Eagle Grove," Blunt said. "Two warehouses, parking lot, fenced perimeter."

"Mercy Creek has three warehouses," KD said.

"More volume of supplies because of the proximity to I-80?"

"Who knows? I'd like to get a look inside."

They drove over to R&G's elementary school job site. A few work trucks were still parked along the shoulder of the road. Weeds grew from the dirt piles that had been bulldozed to one side. The concrete forms on the footings were still in place, but the concrete, rebar standing from its surface, looked hard. "They're going to be here a while," Blunt said.

"Which makes it the perfect cover for running trucks up and down Interstate 35. Ready to go over to the casino?"

The lights were flashing red and yellow on the signage outside the Double Nickel Casino Resort when they pulled into the mostly full parking lot. They checked in at the hotel reception desk and took their bags up to their adjoining rooms on the fourth floor before they came back down to the lobby. People were milling about, waiting, checking in, or strolling straight into the gaming area. KD and Blunt walked through a room of slot machines to get to a wide hallway—restaurants to the right and a ballroom on the left. A wedding party and a photographer were stopped in front of a fountain. KD and Blunt moved along nonchalantly, looking but not looking, trailing other groups of guests, making the rounds, hoping to spot Jimmy Crowder. He wasn't in any of the restaurants or the convenience store. He wasn't playing poker or craps. They finally spotted him at a two-dollar blackjack table.

They sat down on stools at a nearby bar where they could see his back. KD ordered a diet Coke and Blunt ordered a beer.

"Wonder how he's doing?" Blunt asked.

"You a gambling man?"

"Not since I've been married. Used to play cards on deployment to pass the time, you know, friendly game, but I even gave that up. You?"

"Never interested me. Besides, when you're in charge you can't take money from subordinates."

"True enough."

Crowder got up and started strolling through the casino, eyeing women who were showing skin, but he eventually made his way to the elevators. "He got off on the seventh floor," Blunt said.

"Wonder if he's turned in for the night."

"It's still early."

"If he's driving tomorrow, he might be out of here at 6:00 a.m."

They sat down on a sofa in the lobby and watched the elevators. People came down and got out and strolled through to the gaming tables, and people with luggage got in and went up.

KD turned to Blunt and smiled. "Don't look. There's a cowboy at your ten o'clock—jeans, boots, country and western sportscoat. I think he's been tailing us."

"How long?"

"Not sure."

"Let's go outside, see if he follows."

They went out the front doors and started across the brightly lit parking lot. When they were well away from the building, the cowboy hollered after them. "Wait up."

KD and Blunt studied him as he hurried toward them. There was a pistol on his hip under his sportscoat. KD stepped away from Blunt to form a triangle with the cowboy.

"Can we do something for you?" Blunt asked.

"Why are you following Jimmy Crowder?"

"Who's he?"

"The guy you trailed from the blackjack table."

KD smiled. "We don't know who you're talking about."

The cowboy held up his left hand and put his right hand inside his coat. "I'm reaching for my ID." He pulled out a Texas Ranger badge. "Sergeant Tommy Sullivan."

KD nodded to Blunt, and they showed Sullivan their NDA IDs.

"Now that we know we're all on the same side, why are you following Jimmy Crowder?"

"Just checking up on him," KD said.

"Why's that?"

"What's your interest, Sergeant?"

"I think he's linked to a case I'm working."

"It's the same for us," KD replied.

Sullivan studied their faces for a moment. "Philip Richards?"

"You knew him?"

"Philips was a good man," Sullivan said. "We worked together a couple of times. Do you know anything about what happened to him?"

"Just that nobody can be trusted," KD replied.

Sullivan nodded. "It's the worst sort of mess. Video surveillance and wire taps lost or erased. Witnesses missing. Local, state, and federal officials who don't seem to have a clue as to what's going on."

"That bad?"

"Kinfolk who get in the way disappear. It has a way of focusing the mind."

"Guns moving south?"

"And drugs moving north. Heroin and meth. It's nothing new. Why's the NDA involved?"

"Counterterrorism. Hoping what you've got is just regular, garden-variety crime, so we can get back to the office."

"What's Crowder gotten himself into?"

"Other than all his friends murdered? We don't know yet."

Blunt handed Sullivan a business card. "Give us a call if you learn anything that might interest us."

They watched him cut across the parking lot to a white Bronco. "So what do you think," Blunt asked, "dirty or stupid?"

"Maybe both," KD replied. "He spotted us, fed us a line, wasn't pissed off when we didn't tell him anything. We'll have to keep an eye out for him."

They walked back toward the casino. "We've got to know when Jimmy leaves," KD said.

"I'll take the first shift," Blunt said.

"We'll switch out every six hours."

. . .

SULLIVAN REACHED across to the glove box of his Bronco and got out a burner phone. "Mr. Granger? I talked with the NDA investigators. Richards was the mole, just like you thought."

"That's not news. Did you find out anything else?"

"They say they're on a counter-terrorism mission."

"I've heard that before."

"They were following Crowder. He doesn't know they're here."

"Why exactly am I paying you, Tommy? For a Texas Ranger, you don't seem to be very good at finding things out."

"I can't be obvious, Mr. Granger. I meet with them two or three more times, I'll know what they know. I could check with people I trust at the highway patrol or the FBI, if that's what you want. See what they know about these two."

"No, I don't want you to involve anyone else. Just keep an eye out."

"Yes, sir."

SHORTLY AFTER 6:00 A.M., Jimmy Crowder checked out of the hotel and drove the Dodge Dart back to the R&G warehouses. Rocky was sitting behind his desk, stirring two creamers into his coffee.

"Hey, Jimmy, ready to roll?"

"I've been ready."

"Your trailer is in slot five. Your cab's already hooked on." Rocky pulled the spoon out of his coffee, licked it, and set it on a paper napkin. Then he pulled some pages of paperwork from his outbox. "Here's the bill of lading."

Crowder glanced at the first page. "All the way home." He grinned. "Anything else?"

"Drive safe."

Jimmy checked the fifth wheel and the linkage between his cab and the trailer before he climbed up into the driver's seat. It was fifteen minutes to seven. Eighteen hours to get home. He could drive eleven hours today, so he'd have to stop at a quarter to six if he didn't take any breaks. That would leave seven hours for tomorrow. If he started around 6:00 a.m., he could be home by 1:00 p.m. Roslyn didn't get off until 4:00. Plenty of time to rest and get cleaned up. He drove out of the gates and headed toward the interstate.

KD AND BLUNT fell in behind Crowder as he got onto Interstate 35, Blunt behind the wheel of their rented Chevy. The morning traffic was steady, moving fast. The day promised to be clear.

"Wonder what's in that shipping container he's hauling," KD said.

"Guess we'll have to take a look," Blunt replied.

Crowder shifted into the left lane and passed two cars. "He's not wasting any time," KD said.

"He's in a hurry to get home."

KD yawned. "Wish I'd had time to take a shower and get some coffee."

"I've got caffeine pills."

"Are you serious?"

"You can do without, or you can take a couple. In the bag on the back floorboard. Hand me a granola bar while you're at it."

"What did you buy?"

"Water, snacks, No Doze. We don't know when we're going to get to stop. He probably won't need fuel. Is he going to follow the law on how many hours he's allowed to drive in a day, or has he got a work-around?"

KD passed out bottles of water and handed Blunt a granola bar.

"Where did that come from?"

"Convenience store in the casino."

"How old do you think it is?"

"Don't know and I'm not going to look."

KD took two No Doze and drank some water. "Care if I turn on the radio?"

"Knock yourself out."

KD mapped out the interstate rest stops and the truck stops on her map app so that they could drive well behind Crowder on the open road and pull into visual range of his semitruck when they neared a potential off-ramp.

At 12:30 p.m., Crowder pulled into a Drive America Truck Plaza just north of Dallas. KD and Blunt followed him into the parking lot and parked where they had a good view of his tractor-trailer rig. Crowder got out of his cab and rushed into the building. "Now's our chance," KD said. "You want to play tag or take a look?"

Blunt pulled a quarter from his pocket. "I'll flip you for it." He flipped the coin.

"Heads," she said.

He caught the coin. "Heads it is."

"I'm on Crowder."

She climbed out of the Chevy. The parking lot was busy with people gassing up cars or fueling trucks. Truckers in work clothes and billed caps mixed with families trying to corral their children as they came in and out of the building. KD trailed into the convenience store behind a dad and two grader schoolers who were directly in front of her. Once inside, the family headed toward the restrooms in the hallway between the convenience store and the restaurant. KD glanced down the aisles. No Crowder. She moved to the chip aisle, where she had a clear view of the men's restroom door. Crowder came out and turned toward the restaurant. She pulled out her phone as she watched him sit down at a table. She speed-dialed Blunt. "He's sitting in the restaurant."

BLUNT, wearing blue coveralls and a ball cap, was standing beside Crowder's trailer, a shipping container with R&G painted on the side. He had his phone up to his ear. "Keep talking."

He walked around to the rear and stepped up onto the back of the trailer.

"He's looking at a menu," KD said.

"Call me when he leaves."

Blunt picked the padlock on the latch and opened the door to the shipping container just enough to slip inside. He took a flashlight out of his back pocket. Drywall was stacked to the roof on the left side of the container. Interior door kits in their factory packaging were tied in on the right, leaving a foot-wide aisle down the middle. Blunt inched his way to the other end of the container. Boxes of drywall screws and door hardware were stacked behind the interior doors. He shifted two boxes out of the way and found a two-foot by two-foot door shut with a screw. He took out his pocketknife and used the blade as a screwdriver. When he opened the door, he found plastic-wrapped bricks of what appeared to be drugs. He took out his phone. "Hidden compartment loaded with what I'm guessing is drugs."

"He's almost done with his sandwich."

Blunt screwed the door shut, put the boxes back in front of it, and inched his way back out of the container. He took out his phone as he walked away from Crowder's semitruck.

"I'm on the ground."

"Great. Crowder is at the counter, paying. After he leaves, come inside."

Blunt ended the call and took a picture of the trailer license plate before he crossed the parking lot back to their car, where he took off his coveralls and ball cap and put them in the trunk. He was hiding behind the open trunk lid when Crowder hurried out to his truck and climbed inside.

As Crowder drove toward the parking lot exit, Blunt went inside the building. KD was waiting by the door.

"Definitely drugs?" KD asked.

Blunt described what he had seen. "What do you want to do?"

"Let's call Tina, give her the information and have her contact the Eagle County, Oklahoma, sheriff's department. Then we'll see what happens."

"We can't let him get too far ahead."

"I know. He might drop the drugs somewhere along the way, and then we wouldn't learn anything about the Eagle County sheriffs."

KD called Tina, then they went to the restroom, bought some prepackaged sandwiches and bottled iced tea in the convenience store, and gassed up their car. KD got behind the wheel. She caught up to Crowder about thirty minutes later.

"No rest stops before the Oklahoma border," Blunt said. "Then it's about an hour to Eagle Grove."

"Could you unwrap a sandwich for me?" KD asked.

"What kind?"

"Ham and cheese."

He found the sandwich in the sack, tore off cellophane, and handed it to her on a napkin. She lay it in her lap. "He's driving steady."

"Wonder if he knows about the drugs?" Blunt asked.

KD glanced at him.

"He wouldn't need to know, would he? He's driving building materials. That's what he's paid to do. He lives like a guy who's living on a truckdriver's pay."

"Might have a safety deposit box full of cash."

"He's a kid. Could he really resist the temptation? He'd have to spend something even if he was hiding it from his girl. Fancy boots. A car that's just a little too nice. Maybe he'd give her a ring that was a little too expensive, claim he bought off a guy at a truck stop."

"Speaking from personal knowledge?"

"Speaking as the father of teenagers. If this guy knows about the guns and drugs, he isn't benefiting."

"Taking the risk without the reward? That doesn't make sense."

"Maybe he's not supposed to know because he's the sheriff's son."

"You're not going to get me to feel sorry for him."

"Not wanting you to feel sorry for him. Just talking."

At 3:45 p.m., they were driving by the first exit into Eagle Grove. There were no police in sight. Second exit, the same. By the time they rolled by the third exit, it was clear that nothing was going to happen.

"Call Tina," KD said.

Blunt speed-dialed her number. "Hey, Tina, I've got you on speaker with KD. You spoke with the Sheriff in Eagle Grove?"

"Yes. He took the information and thanked me. Sounded like he was serious about stopping the truck. He didn't come through?"

"Didn't even pretend to try."

HENRY GRANGER WAS in his office at the R&G warehouses meeting with Mateo Smits and Rudy Gomez when the Eagle County sheriff called. He put the call on speaker.

"Mr. Granger, I got a call from the National Defense Agency in Washington, DC, that one of your trucks was hauling narcotics, so I thought I should look into it personally."

"Go on."

"I sat in an undercover car with its hood up on the shoulder of the interstate by the last exit into Eagle Grove and watched your truck drive by. I didn't see any other law enforcement, so I'm thinking we're the only ones the NDA called."

"What are you going to do?"

"My logs will show that the tip must have been bad. That we had three cruisers watching the interstate and didn't see any trucks matching the description the NDA gave us."

"Thanks, Sheriff." Granger ended the call.

"Beating the woman didn't convince those NDA assholes to back off," Smits said.

"Maybe it's time to put them in the ground," Gomez added.

"Still too much trouble," Granger replied. "Our Mexican friends want us to keep a low profile. They're our bread and butter, so that's our priority. The NDA investigators might still be sniffing around, they might have searched the trailer and found the heroin, but for whatever reason, it looks like they didn't tell anybody except the Eagle County Sheriff."

"Maybe they wanted to find out if the sheriff would stop the truck. Maybe he just implicated himself," Smits said.

"Maybe, but where is their evidence? They've got no way to prove the Eagle County Sheriff didn't take the tip seriously."

"Maybe Crowder's helping them," Gomez said.

"He's not going to put his family and his future at risk. No, he's pissed off about his friends being killed, but he won't turn against his father."

"Should we pull the dope at a rest stop?" Gomez continued.

"We're not doing anything as long as they might be watching. We don't want them to know that we know."

"So what do you want to do about the investigators?"

"For now? Keep them under surveillance. Keep them from finding out anything else. But if we can't stay ahead of them, we might have to reassess our situation and risk upsetting Mr. Juarez."

KD AND BLUNT followed Crowder up Interstate 35 into Kansas, where he pulled into a truck stop near Wichita at about 6:30 p.m. and drove around into the overnight parking area. A few minutes later, he got out of his cab and went into the restaurant.

"So he's following the regs and parking overnight," Blunt said.

"We can't let that trailer out of our sight. This could be the place the cartel collects the drugs."

"I know. It's going to be a long night. You've been driving. Let me go to the can real quick, and then I take the first shift."

After Blunt got back, KD went into the convenience store side of the building, used the ladies' room, and then washed her face and hands. A quick glance into the restaurant told her that Crowder was taking his time, watching the news on the big screen TV while he ate his supper. KD bought two more prepackaged sandwiches and went back to the car, where she gave one to Blunt. After she ate, she lay down in the back seat. "Restaurant is open all night. Wake me up at 10:00 so I can get a hot meal before my shift."

At 10:00 p.m., Blunt called to her from the front. She rolled up in the seat and rubbed her eyes. "Anything happen?"

"Crowder got into his cab about a quarter to eight. It's been quiet since then."

"I'll be back in a bit."

KD went into the restaurant side of the building. The one waitress on duty, a middle-age woman wearing a cornflower-colored uniform, sat on a stool at the counter. She looked up from her phone. KD walked up to her. "I want two eggs scrambled, two pancakes, bacon, and coffee. I'm going to the ladies."

When she got back, KD sat at a table near to the counter. The waitress brought her a cup and a thermos pitcher of coffee.

"Thank you."

"You bet. Slow this evening."

"You here all night?"

"Just until midnight."

KD drank coffee while she waited for her food. She expected mediocre, but the eggs were soft, and the pancakes were tender, even if the bacon wasn't quite crispy enough. After she finished, she went to the restroom again before she went back out to the car.

"You're early," Blunt said.

"Go on."

Blunt took off and she sat down in the driver's seat. When he came back, he got in the back seat. At 3:00 a.m., she woke him up and they traded out. At 6:00 a.m., he woke her.

"Crowder's up."

She sat up in her seat.

"He just went into the restaurant."

"Okay, let's hit the head and resupply while he's having his breakfast."

AT 1:20 P.M., Jimmy pulled through the gate at the R&G warehouses in Mercy Creek and parked in the slot beside the building. Sandy Gillingham, a full-figured older woman wearing jeans and a sweatshirt, was sitting at the desk when he came into the office.

"Be right with you," Jimmy said. "Back teeth are floating."

"TMI, Jimmy," she said.

When he came out of the restroom, he came back to the desk and handed her the trailer's bill of lading. "There you go."

"You made good time."

"Needed to get home."

She looked at her computer monitor. "You're off tomorrow."

"Great."

"How you doing, champ?"

"I'm okay. Getting by. Trying not to think about the bad."

"Probably a good idea. Got any plans for the rest of the day?"

"Taking Roslyn to dinner."

"We'll give you a call about your next load."

6

KD let Blunt out in the parking lot at the Holiday Inn
Express. He got into the Camry and followed her to the
Enterprise Rent-A-Car, where she dropped off the Chevy.
Then they rolled through the drive-through of Speed-Away Subs &
Such before they went back to the motel and took the elevator up to
their rooms. They both went into KD's room and sat at the square
table near the window, where they unwrapped their sandwiches.

"Okay," KD said, "what have we learned?"

"Looks like the sheriffs are paid off in Eagle County, Oklahoma,"
Blunt replied.

"As well as down in Comanche Pass, Texas. Although we don't
know if that ranger was telling the truth or shining us on."

"If he was lying, it would have to be even worse than he said."

KD nodded. "And we know the local government here is probably
bought off."

"All three cities have R&G warehouses. Guns are going south, and
drugs are coming north."

"But is R&G a front for the cartel or is it a legitimate company
being used by the cartel? You had a look in the warehouses in Eagle
Grove."

"Everything I saw was legit."

"We need to have a look in the warehouses here."

Blunt ate the last bite of his sub and balled up the wrapper. "We were just plain lucky last time. If we really want to take a good look, we need to know what's going on with their security. Maybe Tina can help."

KD called Tina and put her on speaker. "Hey, Tina. We're back in Mercy Creek. We'd like to get a look into R&G's warehouses. Can you get control of the surveillance cameras?"

"Depends on how they're hooked up. Let me take a look and get back to you."

"Thanks."

"It'll probably take a few hours."

"Give me a call when you know something."

KD ended the call. "I'm taking a nap. We might be in for another long night."

Blunt stood up and grabbed his Coke off the table. "I'll be next door when you need me."

WHEN KD's PHONE RANG, she was lying on top of the bedspread on her bed, fully clothed. She grabbed her phone off the night table. It was 6:20 p.m.

"Hey, Tina," she said. "I'll call you back in a minute."

She went into the bathroom and splashed water on her face. Then she texted Blunt. As soon as he was in the room, she called Tina back with her phone on speaker.

"What have you got for us?"

"There are cameras at the gate and in front of the office entrance, as well as cameras inside the offices and two of the warehouses."

"There are no cameras around the perimeter or on the outside of the warehouses?" Blunt asked.

"None. I hacked into their computer. If they were there and turned off, I'd have seen them."

"What do the cameras show?" KD asked.

"The usual stuff you might expect—workers moving around, security guards on patrol, trucks coming and going, building materials being brought in and shipped out—except they've also got surveillance cameras in the bathrooms."

"Nothing of interest?"

"Not for us."

"And the third warehouse doesn't have cameras?"

"The third warehouse doesn't have any surveillance cameras, phone lines, or computers. There was nothing I could hack into."

"Okay," KD said. "At 10:00 p.m. we need for you to have control of the cameras to keep us off the surveillance footage."

"I'll be waiting for your call."

KD and Blunt went to dinner at the Tall Corn Steakhouse across Johnson Boulevard from the Holiday Inn Express. Blunt ordered a New York strip steak with a baked potato and a side salad. KD ordered a rib eye with mashed potatoes and mixed vegetables. Their server brought their iced teas while they waited on their food.

"What do you think we'll find at the warehouse?" Blunt asked.

"I don't know. I'd love to get into the manager's office, but that's just not possible with all the activity around that warehouse."

"And Tina has the first two warehouses sewn up."

"But the third warehouse—either it's empty, which is why there's no surveillance, or there's something shady going on."

"Or it's empty as far as the company knows, but a crooked shift supervisor or custodian is using it to store drugs or guns in transit."

They stopped talking while their server set their plates in front of them.

"Guns would take up an awful lot of space," KD said.

"Yeah, drugs would be easier to hide," Blunt replied. "I guess we'll find out tonight."

MEANWHILE, Jimmy Crowder and Roslyn were sitting in a booth at Ray Bob's Microbrew. A glassed-in area in the middle of the room showed the gigantic stainless-steel brew pot, while tables and booths filled in around three sides and the bar covered the wall in front of the kitchen. A country and pop mix was piped in via speakers high on the walls. Jimmy was eating a pasta dish and Roslyn was having a dinner salad with grilled tofu. A pitcher of beer sat on the table between them.

"It's good to be home," Crowder said.

"When do you go out again?"

"Not sure. I've got tomorrow off, then they're supposed to call."

"I've got to be at the bank at eight thirty."

"It was nice that your mom wasn't home this afternoon."

Roslyn smiled. "She doesn't care that you're in my room. We're not kids."

"Yeah, but she still wants us to get our own place."

"Doesn't your mom?"

Crowder looked off across the room. Roslyn reached across the table to put her hand on his. "What's up?"

He shook his head. "Just thinking about Pat and Susan. We all worked in the kitchen here in high school."

"I remember. You guys would sneak beer out the back."

He got out his handkerchief and wiped his eyes.

"Maybe we shouldn't have come here," she said.

"No, I'm okay. Life goes on. We're going to work, making love at your mom's in the afternoon, going out to dinner. We're living life and they're all dead. It's not right."

"We didn't do it. I'd give anything if they were all still here."

"I know. Me, too. But somebody did it, and nobody seems to care."

"Well, maybe I shouldn't bring this up," she said. "But maybe Philip was the one the killers were after."

"What do you mean?"

"I don't know. He just turned up in town, sweet-talking everyone. Had an apartment and a telecommute job that didn't quite make sense. Always had time to hang out. And he was sleeping with Susan behind Pat's back."

"We don't know that for a fact."

"Come on, you know it was true. And that's not how a friend treats a friend. Not a real friend. Maybe he was involved with drugs."

"That's the kind of gossip people are making up about Pat and Susan, Mike, and Billy."

"Well, I know it wasn't one of them. Hasn't your dad found out anything?"

"He just says it all takes time. But I think it's all going to be swept under the rug."

"Why? Why would he do that?"

"I don't know. I can't say." He drank some beer. "I'm sorry I brought it up. Let's talk about something else."

AT NINE THIRTY, KD and Blunt were driving down Johnson Boulevard, headed into town. "Think we got a tail," Blunt said. "White Ford truck. Two cars back."

KD looked over her shoulder from the passenger seat. "Take the first right."

Blunt turned right at the traffic light. The truck followed them. "Take a left into the neighborhood."

Blunt turned left. The truck followed him.

"You're right," KD said. "They are tailing us, and they're not very good at it."

Blunt raced down the street, took another right, spotted a two-story house with all the lights off, slid into the driveway, and turned his headlights off. The truck drove by. Blunt backed out and drove back to Johnson Boulevard.

"They'll be back in a minute," KD said.

Blunt sped down the boulevard past two intersections, took a left into a neighborhood, drove three blocks, and took another left. Then he parked on the side of the street in front of an apartment building. "Let's give them a couple of minutes to realize they've lost us."

A few minutes later, he drove back down to Johnson Boulevard, took a left toward downtown, and took a right onto Roosevelt Street to take them down to the industrial area, where they parked on Davis

Street, a block away from R&G's perimeter fence, just as they had before. The businesses were all closed, and no one was on the street. KD called Tina. "We're ready to go."

"I've got you."

KD slipped a small backpack onto her shoulders. She and Blunt put on comms sets. "Check," she said.

"All good," Tina replied.

They snuck down the alley between A-1 Home Heating and Cooling and City Recycling, climbed the R&G fence, and dropped down into the dark parking lot, where they crept over to the cover of four parked semitrucks. KD motioned toward the back of the first warehouse. As she and Blunt were starting to move along the wall, Tina came on the comms. "Two security guards just came out of the offices."

KD and Blunt scurried back to the cover of the semitrucks and waited. Two men in blue uniforms strolled by between the semitrucks and the fence, chatting amiably, and then turned to go around the back of the building. KD and Blunt moved along the wall, glancing through the windows into the darkened warehouse as they went, but they couldn't see anything. At the corner, they waited for the security guards to turn back toward the front. "Okay," KD said into her comms, "what have you got?"

"No activity in warehouse one or two," Tina replied.

KD and Blunt scurried along the back of the building, past a garage door and a utility door, Blunt in the lead. At the corner, he glanced across the alley at warehouse two. It was dark in the building. There was no sign of the security guards. They rushed across the alley to the back of warehouse two. As they moved along the back of that building, they heard the motorized front gates roll open and a semitruck enter the parking lot. They sat with their backs against the wall. "Tina," KD said, "truck just entered the compound."

"I saw it come through the gate. Sit tight, truck's in a blind spot. Okay, the driver is going into the offices at warehouse one. I'm switching inside. He's handing over the bill of lading. Hang on. The manager is making a phone call on a landline. I'm going to listen."

The comms were quiet for a minute. "It's nothing," Tina said. "The driver is going home, and the security guards are back at the office."

After they heard the front gate open and close, KD and Blunt moved down to the corner of warehouse two that was closest to warehouse three. Light peeked from the edges of the heavy blinds that covered the windows.

"Tina," KD said. "You've got nothing on warehouse three?"

"No cameras, no tech I could hack."

"The lights are on."

"Good luck."

KD and Blunt crept across the alley to the back of warehouse three. Blunt took off his comms set and put his ear against the wall, but he couldn't hear any noise from inside the building. "Nothing," he said.

They moved down to the garage doors. KD pulled a snake camera from her backpack and pushed it under the door gasket. The monitor showed that the space was brightly lit. There were boxes stacked close by and steel tables in the distance. Blunt watched over her shoulder. No people.

KD and Blunt glanced at each other. "Try the door," KD said. She retrieved the snake camera and put it back in her backpack.

Blunt picked the lock on the utility door and eased it open. They slipped inside. Past the steel tables they'd seen on the monitor, sheets of plastic hung down to create a clean room. Inside that space were steel tables set end to end, digital scales, boxes of plastic bags and plastic film, and large rolls of shipping tape set in heavy-duty dispensers.

"You could eat off the floor in there," KD whispered.

Blunt gestured toward the door at the end of the room.

KD used the snake camera again. The next room was also well lit. No one was there. Blunt opened the door. On one side of the room was an eight-foot-long folding table. A money counting machine sat out on one end. On the other side of the room, guns sat out on shelves that ran from the floor to the ceiling—revolvers, automatic pistols, shotguns, and assault rifles of every major brand. Blunt glanced from the table to the shelves. "Where's the money and where're the drugs?"

There was another door at the end of this room. KD ran the snake under it, but the next room was dark.

"No one's here," Blunt said. "I guess they leave the lights on all the time."

"Looks like the cartel doesn't have to hide anything from R&G," KD replied.

"Anything else you want to see?"

"Let's get out of here."

They went back through the building and out the back. Blunt relocked the door. The parking lot was quiet except for singing crickets and distant road noise.

"Tina," KD said. "What's it look like?"

"I haven't seen anyone outside the office or at the front gate. The security guards should be making their rounds in a few minutes."

KD and Blunt snuck back to the parked semitrucks, where they hid until the security guards disappeared around the back of the first warehouse. Then they scurried across the parking lot to the fence and climbed over.

"Tina," KD said. "Thanks. We're all done."

"Glad to help."

KD and Blunt took off their comms sets and pulled off their gloves as they walked back down the alley toward their car. "So the cartel isn't using R&G, the cartel *is* R&G," KD said.

"And this looks like their major distribution node from Interstate 35 to Interstate 80."

"They bring the drugs here, cut them, ship them out. Chicago, Denver, Minneapolis, Kansas City all within range."

"Could be going anywhere," Blunt replied.

"And the money and guns come back to be shipped south."

"No muss, no fuss, because they own the highway all the way down to Comanche Pass."

KD used the Camry's key fob to open the doors. "And when a

mistake was made, and a shipment of guns was confiscated, they reacted swiftly and brutally."

"Just making sure everyone knows who's who."

"But they didn't kill me when they had the chance. Why?"

"Dead kids being found was a mistake. They're already drawing too much attention. Bad for business."

"So if we push them hard enough . . ."

"We've got to watch our backs, Doc."

GRANGER ENDED the call and put the burner phone in his shirt pocket. He turned to Smits in the passenger seat of the Escalade. "The NDA agents made your guys and lost them."

"They're professionals, Henry. They're trained to spot a tail."

"We've played with them too long. They've been down to Eagle Grove and Comanche Pass. We don't know what they know."

"That's what I've been saying."

"Find out where they went after your guys lost them."

"How?"

"Whose town is this? They parked somewhere. They went in somewhere. Talk to everyone. A junky is bound to have seen them. Or a deputy. Make them earn their pay."

THE NEXT MORNING, KD and Blunt were gathered in KD's motel room on an encrypted video call with Assistant Director Garcia. "Okay, so city and county officials in Mercy Creek seem to be wealthier than they should be. KD was kidnapped by persons unknown. You've talked to a Texas Ranger who might be on the take. And you've got a theory that connects the five murders to the cartel. But let's face it, that's not much of a court case."

"But what about the drug shipment?" Blunt asked.

"You followed drugs being transported in a R&G semitruck from Comanche Pass, Texas, to Mercy Creek, Iowa. That's solid work. But you don't have the drugs, so you can't prove they were drugs and not something else."

"And the warehouse?"

"By the time the FBI gets there with a warrant, will it still be set up to package drugs, count money, and store weapons? Added to the gun bust and the five murders, your investigation suggests that a drug cartel has corrupted the law enforcement and government officials in at least three cities and seems to have control of a shipping route running from Mexico into Iowa, but you've got no concrete proof— no physical evidence and no witnesses."

Blunt cut in. "Can you put a drone on the warehouse?"

"Not without alerting the regional authorities, which would be the same as telling Granger, if they're in his pocket," Garcia replied.

"So what do you want us to do?" KD asked.

"You stay in place. I'll get in touch with the Counter Terrorist Task-force, see if they think this is enough evidence for them to move forward."

GRANGER WAS SITTING in his office at the warehouse complex, going over a report detailing the amount of construction materials they'd need for their legitimate projects over the next quarter, when Smits stepped into the room.

"Close the door," Granger said.

Smits closed the door and sat down in the straight-back chair facing Granger's desk.

"Well?"

Smits spoke to the carpet in front of the desk. "The NDA agents were parked on Davis Street."

"Last night?"

He nodded.

"You saying they came in here? Who was at the desk?"

He looked up at Granger's face. "The old man."

"Jessup? Nobody came by him. What about the guards?"

"They didn't report anything."

"What do the surveillance cameras show?"

"One truck came through the gate. It was expected. Driver went into the office. Went home. No one went into warehouse one or two."

"But they were definitely parked on Davis Street?"

Smits nodded.

"Have the tech guy look through the surveillance feeds for tampering and have someone take a look in the NDA agents' motel rooms."

"Gotcha." Smits scooted up out of the chair.

Granger turned back to the report on his computer, but he couldn't focus on the details. He'd been told to use a light touch, to stay out of the newspapers, to wait them out, all of which hadn't done any good at all. He might have to risk getting rid of them. And if he had to, he needed to make sure that the bodies were taken far away and put deep in the ground.

"YOU THINK THIS WILL WORK?" Blunt asked.

"We need cooperating witnesses. Jimmy Crowder's been driving contraband up and down I-35 for the R&G cartel. I think he's been fooling himself, that he's been willfully ignoring what's right in front of his eyes, and that if we can open his eyes, we can get him to help us."

"But can you bring him around?"

"We'll see."

KD and Blunt were parked on the street half a block down from the Billings house when Roslyn hurried down the front steps, got into her car, and drove off.

Blunt glanced at his watch. "If she gets stopped by a red light, she'll be late for work."

"Let's go," KD said.

They walked up on the porch. Blunt banged on the door. No one came. He looked through the sidelight, saw no one, rang the doorbell and banged some more. Finally, Jimmy Crowder, pants, T-shirt, bare feet, his hair tousled, opened the door.

"Morning, Jimmy," KD said.

"What do you want?"

"Can we come in?"

He held the door open for them. "Come on into the living room. I'll be back in a second."

They walked into the living room. Sofa, two chairs, TV on the wall, a fireplace in between two windows that looked out on the backyard. Jimmy came back with his hair combed and wearing a buttoned shirt.

"Why are you here?"

"We want to solve the murders," Blunt said. "Do you want to solve the murders?"

"You know Goddamn well I want the murders solved. They were my friends. All my friends."

"You know more than you're telling us, Jimmy," KD said.

"What are you talking about?"

"What do you haul for R&G?"

"Building materials."

"So you think that Susan sleeping with Philip behind Pat's back had nothing to do with them being killed?"

"What are you talking about?"

"You don't think that their pillow talk might have led to that shipment of guns getting busted?"

"Are you saying Pat knew he was carrying guns? That he told Susan and Susan told Philip and Philip—what? Told the FBI?"

KD nodded her head. "That's exactly what I'm saying."

"That's insane."

"Is it? Is it insane? Or does it explain everything?"

"Pat was a truckdriver."

"Pat had too much money in his bank account for a truckdriver."

"He was living at home. He was cheap as hell. Maybe he was saving up to get married and make a down payment on buying a house. That's why I've got savings."

"Who was he going to marry?"

"Susan."

"Stop it. Just listen to yourself. He wasn't going to marry Susan for the same reason you broke up with her. He couldn't trust her."

"Then why didn't he break up with her?"

"Because he had nothing better to do. Because he didn't want to mess up the gang. How do I know?"

"I don't believe you."

"Yes, you do. You know I'm right. You know Pat was making a lot more money that you."

"How?"

"Smuggling guns and drugs for Henry Granger's cartel."

"Get out of here."

"Think about it."

"Out!"

Crowder pushed them toward the door and slammed it behind them. As they started down the steps, Blunt said, "That went well."

"He's going to come around," KD replied.

"You sure about that?"

"Why do you think he got so mad? I poked a sore spot."

"Maybe he's just going to put on a Band-Aid."

JIMMY PUSHED BACK the edge of the curtain to the living room window with the back of his hand and watched Thorne and Blunt walk down the sidewalk and get into their car. Was that how Pat really felt about Susan? Had he just been too lazy to leave her? Had she been in the midst of moving on to Philip?

He sat down on the sofa and put his head in his hands. How had the investigators learned so much? He thought back very carefully through what he had told them. Pat wanting to marry Susan, her not wanting to get married, her and Philip—did he really believe any of it? He'd thought it was true when he'd said it, but now?

He went back to the curtain. Their car was gone. They figured Granger was moving guns and drugs. They figured Pat had been involved. But did they know about anyone else? He'd warned Pat not to put money in the bank, just like his dad had warned him. And he'd been super careful not to spend a penny. So he was probably still in the clear. But even if Pat had left a money trail, even if he told Susan and Susan told Philip, none of them deserved to be murdered. Not over a shipment of guns.

Thorne and Blunt seemed to being finding out more about Granger's business than about who the men were who killed Pat and Susan, Mike, Billy, and Philip. He hoped he hadn't made a mistake answering their questions.

THE NEXT DAY, FBI Special Agent Jennifer Ables stood on the wraparound porch of a white, two-story farmhouse located in a grove of oaks down a gravel road to the south of Mercy Creek. She wore dark-framed glasses, jeans, and a flannel shirt open over a gray T-shirt. Her dusty blonde hair was pulled back in a ponytail. She smiled and waved at the rental agent as she backed her car up to the turn-around spot in front of the detached garage.

After the woman was gone, Ables went into the house and walked through to the kitchen, where she stopped at the sink and looked out the window at the overgrown vegetable garden. She got out her phone. "Boss? I'm at the safehouse. I'll set up the computers today and start buying the cars."

"How much time do you need?" Special Agent Chris Martinez asked.

"Two days, tops."

"Have you seen the NDA agents?"

"I'm staying out of their way, just like you told me to."

GRANGER GOT a call from Smits on his burner phone. "There was nothing in their rooms. The tech guy says he can't be sure, but maybe someone was prowling around in our computer system."

"That's it, then. I'm tired of fooling with them. We have to find out what they know, and we've got to get rid of them. I'm calling the sheriff. You be ready at the jail."

Granger ended the call and input the sheriff's number. "Sheriff? It's Henry."

"What's up?"

"We have to deal with the NDA agents."

"You don't want to do that."

"You're going to do as you're told. Arrest one of them for drunk driving. I don't care which. Take them to the jail. Let my guys in through the loading dock."

"Are you crazy? How am I going to keep that quiet?"

"I'm not arguing with you. You've been spending our money. Time to earn your pay."

7

KD and Blunt were driving around town looking for Jimmy Crowder. He wasn't at the Billings house, or at Poppa Joe's Diner, and his truck wasn't parked in the R&G warehouse parking lot.

"You think he's actually going to admit what he knows?" Blunt asked.

"We've got to keep putting pressure on him."

"Work the guilt?"

"Make him see that he's being used—that he doesn't owe R&G anything. Somebody searched our rooms. They're upping their game. They must be worried we're getting close."

"What about his dad? You think he believes that his dad is dirty?"

"He might think his dad looks the other way, but that's probably all. Hell, we don't even know the extent of the sheriff's involvement. It could be that's all he's doing—him and the rest of the county officials."

KD's phone rang. It was Garcia. "What's up, boss?"

"The FBI's counter terrorist taskforce is beginning to put people in place in Mercy Creek. They don't want to tip off R&G, so they won't be in touch until they're ready to move."

"How long?"

"The next few days. Have you got anything new for me?"

"We're trying to turn Jimmy Crowder."

"Keep me in the loop."

"Will do."

She ended the call.

"A couple more days," Blunt said. "I'll be glad to get out of here."

"You really are a homebody, Blunt."

"Nothing wrong with wanting to sleep in your own bed. Aren't you missing your old man?"

"Frank? He's not really my old man."

"But he'd do until one comes along?"

"You know it's more complicated than that."

A sheriff's cruiser rolled in behind them and turned on its lights. Blunt pulled over in front of a stucco, two-story house. The deputy, a heavy-set man wearing his shirt over his Kevlar vest, came up to the driver's side window.

Blunt lowered the window. "Yes, deputy?"

"License and registration."

"I'm reaching into my back pocket for my license and then across to the glove box for the car rental papers."

KD sat still with her hands in her lap. Another sheriff's cruiser came down the street toward them and parked in front of them.

The deputy took Blunt's license and the car rental packet and went back to his cruiser. The other deputy got out of his vehicle and stood in front of their car with his hand on his holstered service weapon.

"This is a setup," KD said.

"I'm going to do my best to keep from being killed," Blunt replied.

A few minutes later, the first deputy came back. "Step out of the vehicle, sir, and put your hands on the hood."

Blunt got out of the car and put his hands on the hood. "I'm a federal agent. I'm carrying a gun on my right hip, registration is in my wallet, along with my ID."

The second deputy drew his pistol. The first one took Blunt's SIG

Sauer. "Mr. Blunt, you're under arrest for drunk driving." He hand-cuffed Blunt behind his back and led him to the back seat of his cruiser. When he came back to the rental car, he looked across the seat at KD. "Ma'am, step out of the car."

KD got out of the passenger's side.

"Identification, please."

"I don't have to show you any identification. I'm a passenger."

The deputy studied her face for a moment. "Have it your way. We're impounding this car."

As KD stepped back onto the sidewalk, a tow truck came around the corner. The second deputy got in his cruiser and drove away. The first deputy pointed to the Camry. The tow truck operator, an unshaven man in gray coveralls, gave a wave, pulled in front of the Camry, and backed into place. Then he got out and started hooking up the rental car. The first deputy drove away with Blunt.

"Where are you taking this car?" KD asked.

"Impound lot behind the jail. You need a ride?"

"No, I'll be fine."

KD walked off into the neighborhood. The deputy had called the tow truck before he pulled them over. That's the only way it could have gotten here so fast. What was their plan, the Sheriff and Granger? The sheriff could keep Blunt in jail twenty-four hours, claim some sort of paperwork foul-up, not take Garcia's phone calls, but eventually Blunt would have to go before a judge, and there'd be no evidence of alcohol.

So that couldn't be their plan. She still had her gun. She needed a car. She came to the intersection with Fifth Street. There was a Hy-Vee grocery story on the other side of the street. She got out her smartphone and tapped on the car fob mimicking app. She didn't want to do this. Steal somebody's car. But she had to move fast, and she couldn't create a trail by using a taxi or a rideshare. She saw a woman wearing a Hy-Vee uniform get out of a Ford Focus and walk into the building. She strolled up to the Ford, tapped on the Ford option in the app, watched the tiny circle fill in. The car was open and ready to drive. She got in and started the car. Quarter tank of gas.

. . .

THE DEPUTY TRANSPORTING Blunt parked in the lot behind the jail and took Blunt through the loading dock into the processing area of the jail, but there was no one there to fingerprint him or give him a breathalyzer or take any information. Instead, the deputy hustled him down an empty hall and placed him in a cell, his wrists still cuffed behind his back.

"What's going on here?"

The deputy slammed the door shut. Blunt sat on the bench. He had an uneasy feeling. He couldn't be murdered here—not in the jail. But anything short of that was probably on the menu.

The cell door swung open and three guys in street clothes rushed in. He recognized one of them—a stocky Latino with a tightly trimmed mustache—but he didn't know his name. The men swarmed him, punching him in the face and abdomen before they knocked him to the ground and kicked him.

Mustache guy said, "You've been snooping around when you should have been minding your business. We couldn't kill your little bitch before, but times have changed. You're going to tell us everything you know, or they're going to hose what's left of you down the floor drain."

"You've got the wrong guy."

The guy to his right kicked him in the head. The cell door opened. The sheriff stepped into the cell, a sour look on his face. "No more of that. I'm not having that in my jail."

"The boss said we could do what we want."

"Not here you can't."

Mustache guy turned to his friends. "Let's go." They left the cell.

The sheriff grabbed Blunt under one arm and helped him up onto the bench. "You two should have left here after they tuned up your partner."

"You know it doesn't work that way, Sheriff. We follow orders."

"Good luck with that."

. . .

KD CIRCLED the jail in the stolen Ford Focus. In the back parking lot, among the parked sheriff's department cruisers, she saw three men wearing casual clothes, not deputies, standing together. One of them, a thickset Latino with a mustache, was on the phone. She parked in the alley next to a dumpster where she could watch them. Then she took out her phone and called the jail. "Could I speak to Jeffery Blunt? He was recently brought to the jail."

"I'm sorry, I don't have any record of anyone by that name being brought in."

"Are you sure?"

"Absolutely."

She ended the call. Was Blunt in the jail? She called Tina.

"What's up?"

"Can you find Blunt's phone?"

"Give me a second." The line was quiet. "GPS says his phone is in the Teague County Jail. Do you need assistance?"

"I'm not sure yet."

KD ended the call. The FBI was almost set up. She didn't want to risk spooking Granger by doing anything official if she didn't have to. She studied the mustached Latino talking on the phone. Deputy arresting Blunt on trumped-up charges, Blunt not in the jail database —this guy and his crew had to be a part of it. She wasn't going to let them out of her sight.

MEANWHILE, Granger sat in his office, holding his burner phone to his ear, listening to Gomez.

"Sheriff told us we couldn't work on the guy at the jail."

"And you haven't learned anything?"

"We didn't have enough time to find out anything yet. We were just getting started."

"Where are you now?"

"In the parking lot."

"Stay there. I'll call back in a minute."

Granger ended that call and speed-dialed the sheriff.

"I've been expecting this call," the sheriff said.

"What part of cooperating don't you understand?"

"We collected him for you. That's enough cooperation. I'm not letting your guys beat a federal agent to death in my jail. That's way out of bounds. Get him out of here and do what you want."

Granger ended the call. It was a hell of a time for the sheriff to grow a pair. After they dealt with the NDA, and everything went back to normal, maybe it would be time to make sure the sheriff knew his place. He called Gomez.

"Yeah, boss."

"Bag the guy and take him out to the Griggs place. Then collect the woman."

Granger put the burner phone in his pants pocket. He should have moved on the NDA agents a long time ago. Holding back, even for Mr. Juarez, had been a mistake. The sheriff would never have challenged him before, but now he thought he had a voice. That was all going to change now. Everyone on their payroll was going to know who was boss.

GOMEZ and his guys went back through the double doors, down the empty hallway, and opened the door to Blunt's cell. Blunt was lying on the bench, his face swelling up, bloody drool running down his chin. Gomez's guys grabbed him by his arms and pulled him to his feet. Blunt tried to smile.

"You've just got to be that guy," Gomez said. He put a canvas bag over Blunt's head, and they hustled him back out to the parking lot. The two guys shoved him into the middle of the back seat of their Suburban. Gomez got into the front seat. "Keep his head down."

They drove north out of town through the rolling hills, golden soybeans and dry corn waiting to be combined on either side of the country road. Gomez took a right onto a weedy gravel road that wound through a grove of diseased apple trees until he came to a dilapidated barn. He drove around back and parked in the shade.

The two guys pulled Blunt from the back seat and dragged him into the barn. One of them uncuffed Blunt's wrists.

"Hands in front."

They handcuffed Blunt's wrists in front of him, connected the cuffs to a chain that ran through a pulley overhead, pulled the chain until Blunt's arms were stretched over his head, and then hooked the chain over a bolt attached to a post in the wall. Gomez removed the sack from Blunt's head.

Blunt blinked. "Your private place. Are we going to get intimate?"

Gomez shook his head. "You're an asshole."

"Pliers and torch?" one of the guys asked.

"No, wait a bit. You two stay here. I'll go find that little bitch. He'll talk when we start working on her."

KD CROUCHED DOWN in the weeds at the base of a dying apple tree when she saw the Suburban come around the side of the barn and start down the hill. Three men came out here with Blunt, but she could only see one in the truck. She crept up to the barn and moved along the wall until she found a crack in the siding wide enough to peek through. Blunt, his arms chained up over his head, stood near a center support post. Two guys sat in lawn chairs on the other side of him, one of them looking at his phone.

"Quit playing that game," the other guy said.

"Nothing else to do."

"Walk around the barn. Make sure nobody's coming."

"Why don't you?"

"Okay, I'll keep watch for thirty minutes. Then it's your turn."

"Fair enough."

Lookout Guy got up. KD couldn't see him anymore. She scurried down to the corner of the barn where the siding had rotted through and rolled into the barn. She was lying in a dark space behind a jumble of wire and broken equipment. What to do? If she shot Lookout guy, would Gaming Guy shoot Blunt or charge out after her? She peeked over the top of a wooden crate. Blunt hung from the chain. On the other side of him, Gaming Guy was glued to his phone. She lay back down. Lookout Guy strolled by her on the outside of the wall. She rolled back out, crawled to the corner, and watched Lookout Guy sit down on the ground with his back against the wall so that he could watch the road. These were bad guys, probably planning to torture and murder Blunt. She didn't owe them anything.

She rolled back under the rotted wall. Lookout guy was sitting on the ground at about the middle of the wall, which meant if he turned around and fired straight through the wall, he'd been shooting more or less at Blunt. Gaming Guy hadn't moved an inch. KD snaked her way through the jumble in the back half of the barn. She had to make her move. There was no telling when Suburban Guy would be back.

"Hey, Chris," Lookout guy hollered, "you hungry?"

Gaming guy looked up from his phone. "You think we're going to be here that long?"

"I don't know."

"I'd take a burger."

"Okay."

Gaming Guy went back to his game. KD heard Lookout Guy talking on his phone. When he stopped talking, she rolled out from behind a rusty tiller and shot Gaming Guy in the chest. He fell forward, his phone falling out of his hand. Before he hit the ground, she turned and fired three times through the wall where she thought Lookout Guy must be. Then she scrambled to the place on the wall where the chain was hooked over the bolt and snatched it free. Blunt jerked his arms down hard. The chain rushed through the overhead pulley and snaked into a pile at his feet. He scrambled toward Gaming Guy, who lay on his side by his tipped-over lawn chair, the chain attached to his handcuffs clattering behind him.

KD ran out the door of the barn and rushed around to where she though Lookout Guy should be, but when she came around the corner to the front, he wasn't there. She ran back the way she had come. When she was almost at the door, she saw Lookout Guy hobbling away across the orchard toward the nearest corn-field. She ran after him. He looked over his shoulder and turned, his gun in his hand. She fired first. His shot went awry as he fell. She covered the distance between them and shot him point blank.

She crouched over him and checked his pulse. Dead. She glanced around. She couldn't see anyone. She rolled him over, went through his pockets, took his phone, keys, wallet, and gun, and left him face down.

She trotted back to the barn. Blunt was sitting in Lookout Guy's lawn chair, checking the magazine of Gaming Guy's gun.

"Doc, I didn't doubt for a minute that you'd show up."

"Fuck you, Blunt. It was harder than it looked."

"No matter, my wife will still want to cook you dinner."

"You got that guy's stuff?"

"Wallet and phone? Yeah."

"You're a mess. Can you walk out of here?"

"Your ride down on the road? I can make it that far."

They made their way down the hill through the dying orchard to where KD had hidden the stolen Ford against a bank of bushes on the shoulder of the road. They got in, and KD started down the road. "We can't go back to the motel."

"Hate to lose our gear."

"Can't be helped."

"Where did you get this car?"

"Stole it."

"So we've got to get rid of it."

"Did you learn anything?"

"Sheriff is fed up. There's definite limits to what he's willing to do."

KD handed Blunt her phone. "Give him a call."

Blunt put the phone on speaker. "Sheriff, how are you?"

"You on your own?"

"I'm with my partner."

"I've got to say I'm surprised at your resourcefulness."

"Me, too. I appreciate your help back at the jail."

"You were never at the jail."

"You help us roll up Granger and R&G, and we'll get immunity for you and Jimmy."

"I don't have the slightest idea what you're talking about."

"Have you got anything that will tie Granger to the murders?"

"We're done." The sheriff ended the call.

KD glanced at Blunt. "It was worth a try. Call Garcia."

Blunt speed-dialed Garcia. KD filled her in.

"Wish you could have stayed off their naughty list a little longer. The Counter Terrorist Taskforce has got a team en route, led by FBI Special Agent Chris Martinez. You'll coordinate with them after they arrive."

"Can we trust them?"

"Martinez is a good man. I worked with him a few years ago."

"Okay."

"Stay on the go. Tina will be in touch with your next moves."

WHEN GOMEZ GOT BACK to the Griggs's barn, he had two more guys with him. They found Chris lying on the ground dead and Blunt missing.

"Damn it," Gomez muttered. He went through Chris's pockets. "They cleaned him out. You two check around for Johnny."

The two guys went outside. Gomez got out his phone. "Henry, it's all bad news."

"Let's hear it."

"I couldn't find the woman anywhere. When I got back to the barn, the guy is gone and two of ours are down."

"Clean it up. I mean sparkling. And then come back to the warehouse."

GRANGER SET his burner phone on his desk. All this trouble from some idiot not digging a hole deep enough. The NDA nosing around. Jimmy Crowder acting like a fool. The sheriff unreliable. They needed to find the NDA agents and kill them. He didn't even care anymore if he found out what they knew. Mr. Juarez would be pissed, but as long as he didn't lose the new shipments, he'd be able to smooth it over. He called Smits. "Move the product, the cash, and the guns now."

"Where to?"

"The new place west of town."

"Okay."

"Take six men with you. And don't let them out of your sight."

"I'm on it."

8

KD and Blunt were driving along a county road west of Mercy Creek when Tina called.

"Hey, guys. Go to Midwest Sporting Goods on Maple Avenue. Ask for Chuck. He'll set you up with clothes, weapons, and a clean car."

"What does he know?" Blunt asked.

"He's a little fish on the outer edges of this case. He thinks you're anarchists on the run from the Feds."

"That's almost funny."

"I do my best."

"So he knows we're black and white?"

"Yes. Call me when you leave there. I'm finding you a place to land." She ended the call.

Blunt used the map app on KD's phone to find Midwest Sporting Goods. They drove into town down Fifth Street, through the intersection with Johnson Boulevard, and took a left onto Maple Avenue. Midwest Sporting Goods anchored a strip mall that contained a hair salon, a coffee shop, and a women's clothing store.

KD parked in the corner of the lot away from the surveillance camera, where they wiped down the front seat area of the Ford for fingerprints. "No bloodstains?" KD asked.

"No bloodstains."

They walked in the front door. No one was at the cash register. To the left was clothing, to the right was hunting and fishing equipment. They walked to the pistol display case at the back, where a huge man wearing a black T-shirt stood with his hands behind his back in front of a wall display of rifles.

"What can I do for you?"

"We're looking for Chuck."

"That's me."

"A friend called for us. We need a full set of gear."

Chuck studied the bruises on Blunt's face. "You look like you've seen some trouble."

"We're in a hurry," Blunt replied.

"Pick out the clothes you need and then we'll deal with the rest."

KD and Blunt went into the clothing section, pulled casual clothes, socks, and underwear off hangers, and shoved them in a duffel. When they came back to the counter, Chuck ushered them into the back room. "Here's what I've got for you." He gestured toward two hard cases. KD opened the one on top. An AR-15 assault rifle, a Glock pistol, and several magazines of ammunition sat in impressions in the case.

She nodded her head. "Just what we need."

"So I was told."

She closed the case and passed it to Blunt before she checked the second one. It was the same.

"Hold on," Chuck said. He looked on his smartphone. "Okay. Your payment came through. Let's go out back."

He led them out a steel security door into the alley behind the building. He gestured toward a white Toyota RAV4. "There's your ride." He handed Blunt the key fob.

"Is it clean?"

"As a whistle."

"Thank you, my friend."

"Hey, I don't do politics. I'm just a businessman."

Blunt used the fob to open the liftback. They put the hard cases and duffel in the cargo area before they got into the front, Blunt in the driver's seat.

"You sure you're okay to drive?" KD asked.

"They just scuffed me up a little. I'm good."

They drove around the building back into the front parking lot and took a right onto Maple Avenue. KD called Tina. "What have you got for us?"

"I just got off the phone with FBI Special Agent Martinez. I'm texting the GPS coordinates of their safehouse. It's just south of town."

"Thanks. Can we trust Sporting Goods Chuck?"

"I've got his phones and internet tapped."

"So that's a *yes*."

"A qualified yes."

"What's the safehouse?"

"It's a farmhouse. FBI Agent Jennifer Ables is there, setting up shop."

"Thanks."

"No worries."

KD and Blunt followed the GPS coordinates south of town until the county road turned to gravel. "Over there." KD pointed to a white, two-story house with a wraparound porch located down a gravel driveway to their right.

Blunt turned up the driveway. "Ready for trouble?"

"Yeah."

A woman wearing dark-framed glasses came out onto the porch. KD got out of the passenger's side of the RAV4 with her SIG Sauer down at her side.

"You Thorne?" the woman asked.

KD nodded.

"I'm Jennifer Ables."

"What's your boss's name?"

"Martinez."

KD holstered her pistol.

"And yours?"

"Garcia."

Ables nodded. "Good to meet you."

Blunt got out of the driver's side. "Car all right here?"

"Is it clean?"

"Supposed to be."

"Leave it there for now," Ables replied. "Come on in. Need any help?"

"We're good," Blunt said.

KD and Blunt carried in the gun cases and the duffel containing their new clothes and set them on the floor by the front door.

"Make yourselves at home."

"How secure is this place?" Blunt asked.

"No one can come up here without me knowing about it. The computers are up and the perimeter sensors are set. Martinez and the crew will be here tonight. Then you can brief him. In the meantime, you can settle in. I've got work to do. There's food in the kitchen. You can take two bedrooms upstairs."

"I'm going to get cleaned up," Blunt said.

"There a first aid kit in the kitchen, if you need it."

Blunt took the duffel of clothes with him upstairs. KD opened one of the gun cases on the coffee table and started checking the action on the assault rifle.

"Relax," Ables said. "We're not going to have any trouble here."

"I hope so, but I plan to be locked and loaded just in case."

LATER THAT EVENING while Granger was sitting on his back porch reading the *Mercy Creek Times* on his tablet, he felt his burner phone vibrate in his pocket.

"Mr. Juarez. I wasn't expecting to hear from you."

"I had to find out from a contact that the warehouse was compromised."

"We don't know that for a fact. I'm just making sure that nothing interferes with our business."

"I asked you to contain your problem, to keep a low profile, to not do anything to draw suspicion."

"I let the NDA investigators roam as if there was nothing to find. Took extra precautions to hide our loads. There's nothing lower profile than that."

"What about your crew kidnapping the woman agent?"

"We can't operate blind. We had to make sure she didn't know anything."

"And yet the NDA tipped the sheriff in Eagle County."

"And the sheriff tipped me. We've got this under control. The investigators won't find the new warehouse. It's not involved with the shipping business."

"You're running out of chances. If you can't make this work, we'll have to make changes."

"We're going to make this work. Nothing is going to interrupt our business."

Mr. Juarez ended the call.

Granger looked at the phone in his hand. Damn it. The last-chance speech. Juarez thought he wasn't up to the task, but that the situation was still salvageable. Where was he getting his information? And who was he planning on replacing him with? Mateo? Rudy? One of the other guys? He'd show them all why he was the boss.

He called Mateo. "Did you do what I asked?"

"Everything's been moved, Henry. We're all set up at the new location. Adding the building materials to camouflage the loads will be a pain, but otherwise, we're set."

"Great. Now we're ready to deal with the sheriff. Collect Jimmy and his girl. Take them out to the new warehouse. They'll be our collateral to guarantee the sheriff's cooperation finding the NDA agents."

"Sheriff's going to pitch a fit."

"Sheriff's going to pitch a fit? I'm the one pitching the fit. We've been too lenient with him all along. He's going to learn to follow orders, just like everyone else who gets paid."

MEANWHILE, FBI Special Agent Chris Martinez, along with three members of his team, arrived at the farmhouse. After they brought their gear in, everyone gathered in the dining room.

"Agents Thorne and Blunt, I'm Chris Martinez." He pointed to a small woman with short, dark hair, a thin blond guy with a crewcut, and a full-figured woman with a dark ponytail. "This is Lorraine Michaels, Rafe Jones, and Sally Reims. Jennifer Ables you already know." They were all dressed in T-shirts, flannel shirts, and jeans.

KD and Blunt shook hands all around.

"Let's get down to business," Martinez said. "How are we set, Jennifer?"

"The house is stocked. I've got two cars out back for surveillance and the computer system is good to go. I've been in contact with our teams in Eagle Grove and Comanche Pass. As soon as the boss got the FISA warrants, I hacked into the sheriff's department, the public surveillance cameras, and the R&G offices. I'm still working on the unidentified cell phones."

"Good work."

He turned to KD and Blunt. "Fill us in on the specifics."

KD turned to Ables. "Can I borrow that laptop?"

She slid the laptop across the table. KD input her passwords, downloaded a file folder, and opened it to show a file and two more file folders. "Here's the transcript of our investigation, and two folders assembled by our tech people that contain photos of the key players and plans for the warehouses, both here and in Oklahoma and Texas."

Martinez scanned through the files. "This is good stuff. But you didn't have any warrants for the searches you did?"

"Correct."

"So none of that can be used in court. We'll have to chalk it up to a confidential informant."

He clicked on the plans to the warehouses. "Are these accurate?"

"Here in Mercy Creek, yeah. The others are the plans from the original builds, so there might be changes."

"And they were packaging drugs in building three here?"

"Didn't see any drugs, but all the equipment and materials were there," KD said.

"I'm sure a drug dog would be doing his happy dance," Blunt added.

Martinez continued. "In terms of our timeline, they abducted you after you came back from Comanche Pass."

Blunt nodded. "They want to know how much we know. Otherwise, we'd probably already be dead. After we tipped the Eagle County sheriff about a shipment of drugs, that's when they got scared enough to get the sheriff here involved. He's corrupt, but he wouldn't let them murder me at the jail."

"So they know you're on to them, and the sheriff's not completely reliable. They're probably changing things up right now. I'll coordinate with our teams in Eagle Grove and Comanche Pass. My people will put the principals under surveillance, see if we can't catch them with a shipment in transit. You two will hang back here until we have a handle on what's going on."

JIMMY AND ROSLYN were already in bed when they heard pounding on the front door downstairs.

"God, Jimmy," Roslyn said.

"I'll go."

Jimmy pulled on his jeans and went out into the hall. Mrs. Billings, her terrycloth bathrobe wrapped tightly around her, stood in the doorway to her bedroom. "Who's at the door?" she asked.

"I don't know," Jimmy said. "Don't worry, I'll handle it." He went downstairs to the front door. Smits and Gomez were standing on the porch.

"Guys? Really? It's after ten o'clock."

"Get dressed," Smits said. "You and your girl. Mr. Granger wants to talk to both of you."

"How about we stop by the warehouse tomorrow?"

"Now."

"You got nothing to worry about," Gomez added. "You're the sheriff's son, nothing's going to happen to you."

"Why would I be worried?"

"Get a move on," Smits said.

"Okay, okay," Jimmy said.

"We'll be waiting," Smits said.

Jimmy went back up the stairs. "Just a work thing, Mrs. Billings. Sorry."

She closed her bedroom door. He went back into Roslyn's bedroom. "Come on, babe," he said. "You've got to get up."

"Why?"

"Mr. Granger wants us."

"Us? I don't work for him."

Jimmy turned on the light. "I know it doesn't make sense, but Mr. Granger is used to having his way. Do it for me."

"You owe me."

"Okay."

"I'm serious." She stood up out of bed and pulled her nightgown off over her head. "I'm not putting on clean clothes." She picked up her underwear from the floor.

A few minutes later they were on the porch with Smits and Gomez. "We'll take my truck," Jimmy said. "We'll follow you."

"You ride with us," Smits said. "We'll bring you back. Door-to-door service."

They got in the back seat of Smits's crew cab truck. As Smits was backing out of the driveway, Jimmy called his father.

"Hey, Dad."

"Christ," the sheriff said. "What's the emergency?"

"Mr. Granger sent Mateo and Rudy to pick up me and Roslyn."

"Right now?"

"I'm calling from Mateo's truck."

"Okay. I'll take care of it."

Jimmy ended the call.

"What did he say?" Roslyn asked.

"Not to worry."

THE SHERIFF ROLLED out of bed with his phone in his hand.

"What is it, dear?" his wife asked.

"Nothing. I'll be back in a second."

He slipped his feet into his slippers and trudged off down the hall and into the bathroom, where he closed the door. He found Henry Granger's phone number in his contacts and tapped it.

"Sheriff," Granger said.

"What the fuck do you think you're doing?"

"Focusing your mind on the task at hand."

"Which is?"

"Finding those NDA agents."

"So that fella slipped out on you. I told you I was done with that."

"You don't tell me, I tell you. You're going to reach out to all your contacts. You're going to have every deputy beating the bushes. You're going to provide all the help I need."

"I can't do it. You're drawing too much attention."

"I like your son, Sheriff, and I don't want to hurt him. You've been paid. Do your job." He ended the call.

The sheriff sat down on the toilet lid. Henry was scared. He couldn't find Thorne or Blunt. They must know something—no, they must have found something, some hard physical evidence, something that would hold up in court. Henry wouldn't hurt Jimmy or Roslyn. He wasn't crazy stupid yet. So if he just dragged his feet, waited things out, either Henry would eliminate Thorne and Blunt or the Feds would arrest him. Maybe he could find a way to contact Thorne and Blunt, make a deal, play both ends against the middle. Maybe that was his best bet. Unless Henry went off the deep end. Then he'd have to take matters into his own hands.

.   .   .

SMITS DROVE his truck down a potholed country road in the dark somewhere west of town.

"Where are we going?" Jimmy asked.

"No worries," Smits replied. "Mr. Granger has a place out here."

"He's meeting us out here tonight?"

"Jimmy, I just do what I'm told, okay? I'd like to be home in a warm bed just like you."

He drove by some wasteland next to a farm field and turned up a gravel driveway hidden in the woods. As they rolled over a ridge, a warehouse surrounded by a chain-link fence came into view. A pole light shined over the gate and another over the front door. As they approached, the gate in the fence automatically slid open, and Smits drove through and pulled to a stop in front of the warehouse.

"Mr. Granger is waiting inside."

"I don't like this, Jimmy," Roslyn said.

"Is Mr. Granger really out here?" Jimmy asked.

"Don't make this harder than it has to be," Gomez said. "You're getting out of the truck and you're going inside."

"Something's wrong," Roslyn said.

"We don't want to hurt you or your girl, Jimmy," Smits said. "Just come inside and talk to Mr. Granger."

Jimmy squeezed Roslyn's hand. "Okay."

They all got out of the truck. Smits led the way and Gomez followed behind Jimmy and Roslyn. Inside, the outer office was just like the one at the R&G warehouse complex.

"So where is he?" Jimmy asked.

"Down the hall," Smits replied.

Smits opened the first door in the short hallway, and they all walked into a studio apartment. There was a kitchenette at one end, a sofa facing a TV in the middle, and a king-size bed at the other end, where a door led to a bathroom.

"Where's Mr. Granger?" Jimmy asked.

Smits shrugged. "It's not personal, Jimmy. Mr. Granger has business with your dad. You two are staying here until it's settled."

"You can't keep us here," Roslyn said. "That's kidnapping."

"Think of it as a little vacation," Gomez said. "Refrigerator's stocked. I'll come by to check on you, make sure you have everything you need."

"This is crazy, Mateo. Let me call Mr. Granger."

"I can't do that, bro. You want to blame someone, blame your dad. If he'd kept his word, we wouldn't have to do this."

"What was he supposed to do?"

"We're not getting into that."

"My mom's going to go crazy," Roslyn said. "The bank will wonder where I am."

"Call in sick. It'll only be a few days. And Rudy will let you call your mom when he stops by to check on you. Tell her you and Jimmy are taking some time—whatever, I don't care."

"Lie to her?"

"You don't want to tell her the truth."

"What makes you think we won't break out of here as soon as you're gone?" Jimmy asked.

"Don't make it hard on yourselves." Smits replied. "You don't want to be tied in a chair wetting yourself. Cooperate. Next thing you know you'll be back to your lives."

"Which reminds me," Gomez said, "I need your phone and her purse."

"You can't have my purse."

"Do I need to manhandle you and take it?" He looked at Jimmy. "I don't want to put my hands on her, but I will if I have to."

Jimmy gave Gomez his phone. "Give him your purse."

Roslyn handed it over. Gomez looked inside. Her phone was there. "Thank you," he said.

"Relax," Smits said. "No one will harm you here. Eat, drink, watch TV, do whatever you do. Rudy will be by tomorrow afternoon."

Smits and Gomez left the room. Jimmy and Roslyn heard the deadbolt slide home. Roslyn put her hand on her heart. "I think I'm having a panic attack."

"You're hyperventilating." Jimmy searched through the kitchen drawers until he found a paper bag. "Breathe into this."

Roslyn put the bag over her mouth and tried to slow her breathing. After a few minutes, she was breathing normally. "Okay," she said. "That's better." She set the paper bag down on the kitchen counter and walked the length of the room, stopping to look out the window into the dark.

"I'm so sorry I got you into this," Jimmy said.

She sat on the arm of the sofa. "Are we going to try to escape?"

"You heard Mateo. It would just make things worse."

"Why are we here?"

"I don't know."

"Really? Businessmen don't kidnap people. What's your dad got to do with Mr. Granger?"

"I don't know."

"What do you know that you're not telling me?"

"Why would I know anything?"

"You work for Mr. Granger."

"I drive a truck. That's all I do. I don't know anything about his business."

THE NEXT MORNING, the sheriff sat in his office looking at a map of all the real estate listings in the county. He eliminated all the rentals in town. Then he added the location of any R&G properties and any R&G shell company properties he was aware of. Finally, he added the locations of abandoned properties. Henry would be most likely to have Jimmy and Roslyn at a property where he had complete control, which meant an R&G property or a shell company property. One without employees coming and going.

And Thorne and Blunt would most likely be in an abandoned property or a country rental—someplace without neighbors—if they hadn't left the county.

He sipped his coffee. So this was the map of the properties he needed to check out. There were thirty-nine in total. A lot more than he'd expected, but some of them he'd only have to drive by. If he could find out where Jimmy and Roslyn were being held, he'd be able to free them if Henry continued to be unreasonable. If he could find Thorne and Blunt—well, he'd be able to turn them over to Henry or work out a deal with them if it was clear that Henry was on his way out. Plus, him driving all over the county would convince Henry that he was actually trying to help. It was a good plan.

9

Over the next few days, Granger consolidated his drug and gun operations out at the new warehouse and prepared for an FBI raid on the R&G facility in town. Two trust-worthy guys power-washed warehouse three. Smits and his team stayed hidden out at the new warehouse where the drugs and guns were stockpiled. Only Gomez went back and forth, taking food and delivering messages, driving around in circles to make sure he wasn't being followed. The other members of his crew were scouring the county, searching for the NDA agents or anyone who was new and might be an undercover cop.

"We haven't found them," Gomez said. "I think they ran."

"They were inside the R&G warehouses," Granger replied. "They're planning something."

Granger sent semitrucks south and north along I-35, transporting construction materials, but the FBI didn't stop any of the trucks, and his paid-off law enforcement hadn't heard anything through back channels, so it was time to try a few test loads. They ran a utility van carrying one brick of heroin over to Chicago. No problems. Then they brought a semitruck loaded with construction materials to the new warehouse in the middle of the night, loaded a few guns into a secret compartment, and took the truck back to the R&G facility. An R&G driver drove it down to Comanche Pass. Still no problems. And the NDA agents were still nowhere to be found. He couldn't wait any longer. It was time to reopen the pipeline.

MEANWHILE, KD and Blunt stayed in the farmhouse, finalized their report for Garcia, and responded to questions about the players or the town from the FBI agents on surveillance. Four days later, the twenty-four-hour-a-day surveillance paid off. Shortly after 7:00 p.m. Jennifer Ables and Loraine Michaels followed Rudy Gomez's truck down a gravel driveway along some wooded wasteland beside a farm field to a rust-red, sheet-metal building surrounded by a chain-link fence. Gomez got out of the driver's side carrying two large bags from Speed-Away Subs & Such.

Ables and Michaels turned around on the gravel and drove back out to a place on the county road where they could watch the end of the driveway. About thirty minutes later, Gomez, still alone, drove out onto the road and turned right, headed toward town.

Ables and Michaels drove back to the farmhouse. Martinez, KD, and Blunt were sitting in the living room. They described what they'd seen.

"That's the first new place they been to," Michaels said.

"That we know of," Martinez replied. "We're stretched too thin with only two surveillance teams. And it could be anything. Gomez taking dinner to his cousin."

"Chris, this is our first solid lead. We need to have a look inside," Ables said.

Martinez shook his head. "You know what's happened before. We'll need a search warrant based on evidence from the FISA warrant. We go for the search warrant, and Granger'll be tipped off before the judge's signature is dry. We have to know the contraband is there before we go to the judge. We'll only get one opportunity."

"We could take a look," KD said. "And we'll organize the hacking and wiretaps. That way we can be sure there won't be a leak."

"This is a very sensitive situation. We don't want any blowback that could affect the case."

"So no gunfire," Blunt said.

"You can't be discovered at all," Martinez replied. "Anyone who could testify to an illegal entry could quash whatever we find with the subsequent warrant."

"It's your call," KD said.

"This is our best chance to get this case moving," Ables said.

"Okay," Martinez replied. "You can go in. Ables will go with you. She knows our protocols."

"Just as long as we're clear that I'm in charge in the field," KD said.

"You're running the op," Martinez replied.

KD turned to Ables. "What are the GPS coordinates for this warehouse?"

Ables showed her the warehouse on her map app.

"I'll get our people started on hacking the location. For the sake of plausible deniability, I'm leaving you out of this call."

KD and Blunt went out on the porch. KD called Tina. "Hey, I'm texting you a location. I need for you to hack into it right away."

"I'll see what I can do."

KD and Blunt went back into the living room. "Our people are getting started," KD said.

TWO HOURS LATER, Tina called back. "Sorry, guys, no internet, no landline, not even any electricity. Pinging off the nearest cell tower, I can tell there are cell phones out there, but I've got no way in."

"So whatever is there is low tech?" Blunt asked.

"Exactly. Any surveillance goes to an onsite computer. Ditto for the alarm system. Assuming they're on generators."

KD and Blunt carried their gear downstairs to the living room where Ables and the others were waiting. "That warehouse is off the grid, so surveillance and alarms are all local," KD said.

"Which means we can't get control of them," Martinez said, "so this operation is all old school."

"What are you using for weapons?" Ables asked.

"Off the shelf gear we got from a contact," KD said. "We could use comms sets and body armor, though."

"We can help with that," Ables said. She unpacked two plastic crates from a stack in the corner of the room and pulled out three Kevlar vests and three boxes containing communications headsets.

"Sweet," Blunt said.

"The comms sets are all on the same frequency, so they're good to go."

"Excellent." KD turned to Martinez. "We'll use a phone to keep in touch."

KD, Blunt, and Ables drove the white RAV4 northwest from their safehouse, following the map app on KD's phone out to the wooded area by the farm field. Blunt backed the SUV off the county road into a spot among a group of honeysuckle bushes. It was already dark in the woods. "How far?"

"Up the gravel driveway to the other side of the ridge," Ables replied.

"Let's get started," KD said.

Blunt popped the latch on the liftback. They all got out of the RAV4, went around to the back, and put on their Kevlar vests and comms headsets. "Check, check," Ables said.

KD and Blunt nodded. KD speed-dialed Martinez on her smart-phone. "We're on."

"Good luck," he said.

They started up the side of the driveway in the dark, Ables in the lead, their AR-15 rifles in their hands, their pistols holstered on their hips. At the top of the ridge, they could see light peeking around the edges of the windows of the warehouse and one pole light illuminating the front yard. A razor-wire-topped chain-link fence surrounded the compound, and three semitruck cabs attached to shipping containers sat to the right side of the warehouse. KD tapped Ables on the shoulder and pointed off to the right. "We'll cut the fence around back, out of sight of the gate."

They crept through the tall weeds along the tree line until they rounded the corner of the compound. They could hear a gas generator firing close by. "Okay," KD whispered into her comms, "What do you see?"

"Camera on the front corner of the building," Ables said.

"Same with the back," Blunt said. "But look at the angles. Both cameras are set to cover the maximum area, so they can't see what's right under them."

"Blind spot between them?"

"Low to the ground. What do you think, Ables, at about the middle of the closest truck?"

"That sounds right," Ables replied. "And the trailer on the closest truck is blocked by the other trucks."

"So we'll be able to get a look in there on our way in," KD said. "Blunt, on lookout."

They crawled across the open area to the fence. Blunt veered off toward the corner where he could see the front gate and lay down in the grass. Ables pulled a set of wire cutters from the cargo pocket of her pants and clipped through the fence three feet high.

KD heard Blunt on her comms. "Hold."

KD and Ables lay down in the grass, making themselves as flat as possible. They heard footsteps, but they didn't look up. A few minutes later, Blunt whispered, "Clear."

KD and Ables got up on their hands and knees. "How many?" KD asked.

"One. Street clothes and a holstered pistol."

KD nodded at Ables and then held the fence open for her to crawl through. Ables did the same. They scurried across the yard to the first semitruck.

"Blunt?" KD whispered into her comms.

"Clear," he replied.

KD and Ables crept around to the back of the shipping container. The door wasn't locked. KD pushed up on the lever and opened the door a crack. Ables pulled out her penlight and shined it in. Four plastic crates sat in the middle of the trailer. KD boosted herself into the trailer, went to the nearest crate, and lifted the lid. Shotguns wrapped in newspaper. She gave Ables the thumbs up, put the lid back on the crate, and climbed out.

"Guns," she whispered.

They crouched under the truck trailer to stay out of sight of the camera and scurried to the wall of the warehouse. No alarm. No one running out of the warehouse to kill them. They crept along the side of the warehouse until they came to the first window. Light streamed through a gap in the blinds. KD peered in. Three women wearing only their underwear and gym shoes, respirators on their faces and their hair pulled back behind their heads, stood at a long, metal table. The first one was mixing powder in a large metal bowl, the second one was weighing bags of the mixture on a digital scale, and the third one was wrapping the weighed product into bricks. Two men wearing jeans and T-shirts, pistols in their belts and respirators on their faces, stood by the door, watching the women work. KD tapped Ables on the shoulder and motioned toward the next window. As they sneaked along the wall, they heard Blunt on their comms. "Vehicle approaching."

KD and Ables leaned against the wall and waited. They heard a vehicle come to a stop on the other side of the warehouse, the doors slam, and two people talking. Then the warehouse door shut. "All clear," Blunt said.

KD and Ables made their way to the next window, but there was no gap in the blinds. On the third window, the blind was raised a few inches. They crouched and peeked in. They saw the back of a sofa and the top half of a TV against the far wall. Two people sat on the sofa, but all they could see were the backs of their heads.

"Same guy starting around the building to the right," Blunt said.

KD and Ables scurried back the way they'd come. They were lying in the grass outside the fence when the guard walked by on the near side of the warehouse. As soon as the guard went back inside, Blunt crept back to their position, and they all scrambled back to the tree line.

KD called Martinez and put him on speaker. "There are guns in a semitruck in the yard, and they're packaging drugs in the warehouse."

"Anything else?"

"Couldn't risk going inside."

"Ables?"

"Yeah, boss?"

"I'm getting the warrant for R&G's properties. We'll be ready to go by morning. You stay there to keep them under surveillance."

Ables turned to KD. "This is our show now. Everything has to be by the book."

"Absolutely. We'll back you up."

"Appreciate it," she said.

"See you in the morning," Martinez said. He ended the call.

"Let's move to a spot on the tree line that's opposite the front corner," Ables said. "That should give us the best view."

They scurried down the tree line until they came to a fallen oak they could lie behind that offered a good view of the front gate.

"This is the spot," Blunt said.

"Let's settle in," Ables replied.

SMITS SAT in the office at the warehouse, talking on his smartphone. "That's right, Henry. The guns are ready to go. We just need the building materials to fill up the trailer."

"Okay. Send them with the next shipment of interior materials for the school in Comanche Pass. What about our other product?"

"The girls are almost done with the Chicago shipment. It'll be ready tomorrow."

"Send two guys with the load. Have them leave first thing in the morning."

"Are you sure it's time?"

"No one's seen the NDA agents in days. And we haven't had any problems with the test runs. We need to get all our materials out of here. Then if the FBI raids us, we can stop for a few weeks, and we'll be in the clear. Anything else?"

"No."

"I'm counting on you."

"We'll get it done."

Granger ended the call.

Smits put away his phone and went out into the outer office, where two men were sitting on a sofa and a fat man wearing a ball cap was sitting in a recliner. Smits spoke to the fat man. "Randy, one of you guys is going to be walking the yard at all times tonight. Understand?"

Randy nodded.

Smits walked down the hallway, passing by the studio apartment. He couldn't hear Jimmy and Roslyn, but he knew they were in there. He opened the door to the clean room and motioned for Skip to step out.

Skip shut the door behind himself and pulled down his respirator.

"We on schedule?" Smits asked.

"Yeah, all the dope is cut. Melissa will have the last of it packaged in another hour, more or less."

"Great. Joe and Gary will be here at 7:00 a.m. Nobody leaves until they're gone."

"Even the girls?"

"Especially the girls. After they shower, they can hang out in the kitchen if they want, but nobody leaves before Joe and Gary."

"Okay. How much longer are we keeping Jimmy and Roslyn?"

"I don't know."

"The longer they're here, the more likely they'll find out something."

"I know, but Henry is the one who decides."

"Might have to get rid of them."

"It's not your concern. Just keep the girls here until the shipment is gone."

. . .

IN THE STUDIO APARTMENT, Jimmy and Roslyn lay together in the dark in the king-size bed, still awake, listening to the warehouse noises.

"This is crazy," Roslyn whispered. "They're going to kill us, just like they killed Pat and Mike and Susan and Billy."

"And Philip."

"We don't need to go into that again. I still think it was probably his fault."

"Well, whether Philip was at fault or not, Mateo and Rudy are not going to kill us."

"You keep saying that."

"Two reasons. One, we don't know anything."

"Really?"

"Roslyn, I've told you. All I do is drive a truck. And two, if they kill us, they have to kill my dad. It's not going to happen."

She shifted onto her shoulder to look into his eyes. "If we get out of here, I'm leaving town. I'm not waiting for you any longer."

"Babe, I'm with you. As soon as we get out of here, we've leaving. We've got our nest egg. It's always been our plan. We'll go to Des Moines, try it for six months, go somewhere else if we don't like it."

"We've got to get out of here. I can't keep telling my mom that we're moving in together if it's not going to happen."

"I'll talk to my dad in the morning."

"You think Rudy will let you call him? We've been here most of a week."

"Exactly. We've been here, and my dad's been pressuring them to let us go. Something's got to give."

KD, Blunt, and Ables sat through the night, watching the warehouse from behind the tree line, the only movement the guards making their rounds. At 5:30 a.m., a semitruck came through the gate and backed in next to the rig carrying the crates of guns. Five men, including the guards, came out of the warehouse and transferred materials from this semitruck to the one with the guns.

Ables called Martinez to fill him in.

"Okay," he said. "I'll send Lorraine to tail the semi if it leaves. The SWAT team will be there in an hour."

Thirty minutes later, Ables got a call from Agent Michaels. "Hey, Lorraine."

"I'm in place at the bottom of the hill."

"Great. Looks like they're almost done loading the semitruck. I'll call you if it moves."

"Okay."

At 6:35 a.m., two armored cars marked FBI, followed by a black Ford Explorer, rolled over the ridge and down the gravel road to the gate. Martinez, wearing tactical gear and body armor, got out the Explorer with a megaphone.

"Federal agents. We have a warrant to search the premises."

No one came out of the building. The first armored car crashed through the gate, followed by the second one. A dozen FBI agents in body armor swarmed out of the armored cars, broke down the front door, and rushed inside the building. Gunfire erupted from inside. KD, Blunt, and Ables raced down the hill and through the smashed front gate.

SMITS RAN down the hall toward the back of the warehouse, his phone in his hand. Two security guards and a truck driver were right behind him. "Henry. We're being raided."

"Save the dope."

"No time. The FBI is already inside."

Smits put his phone back in his pocket, opened a closet door, found the hidden latch, and pulled up the trap door to the tunnel. He climbed down the steel ladder bolted to the wall and flipped on the light switch. "Last one down, close the trap door."

He ran down the tunnel at a crouch, headed northeast to where the tunnel came out in a barn where a Suburban was parked.

· · ·

KD, Blunt, and Ables rushed around to the back of the warehouse. Three women and two men were running out of a garage-style door toward the fence. Ables went down on one knee and raised her rifle. "On the ground now!"

One of the men pulled a pistol from his belt. Ables fired twice. He fell sideways.

"On the ground," she yelled.

The others got down on their knees and raised their hands over their heads.

Two FBI agents came out the back door. The one in front waved at Ables and then ran over to the fallen man and kicked his gun away.

"Need a medic?" Ables yelled.

The agent shook his head.

His partner disarmed the remaining man and then cuffed the man and the women behind their backs before they led them around the building.

The shooting stopped as abruptly as it had started. In the eerie quiet, all they could hear were FBI agents barking commands.

KD, Blunt, and Ables jogged around to the front of the building. Five men and two women stood beside the building with their hands cuffed behind their backs. Martinez was standing in the yard, talking on his comms. He motioned them over.

"That was quick," KD said.

An agent came out of the building leading Jimmy and Roslyn. "Found these two in a locked room. They claimed they were kidnapped."

"That's the sheriff's son and his girlfriend," KD said. "They've been missing for days."

"Take them to the command center at the courthouse for questioning," Martinez said.

Agent Michaels came around the outside of the warehouse. "We've got it all, boss. Bricks of drugs inside and a shipment of guns in the semi."

"Photograph and collect the evidence. Michaels, you take charge here."

Martinez took out his smartphone and dialed Sheriff Crowder's personal cell number. "Sheriff Crowder? This is FBI Special Agent Chris Martinez. I'm letting you know that we just executed a federal search warrant on two properties in your jurisdiction. Found your son and his girlfriend locked in a room at one of them."

"Are they all right?"

"Yes. We're transporting them to our command center to make a statement, then they'll be released."

"I appreciate that. We been looking for them for five days. Glad they're okay. What did you find?"

"Drugs and guns."

"Why wasn't I informed about the warrant? We'd have been happy to help."

"I'm sure you would, Sheriff, but the timeline got ahead of us."

"I bet."

He ended the call and turned to KD and Blunt. "You two with me."

They got in the Ford Explorer, Martinez driving, KD in the front passenger seat, Blunt in the back.

"Looks like you've got your case," Blunt said.

"It's a great drug case. But the conspiracy? We're a long way from proving that."

KD shifted in her seat. "How did things go down in Eagle Grove and Comanche Pass?"

"There's a gunfight ongoing in Comanche Pass, but it's just a matter of time. Eagle Grove went just like here. R&G is finished. But we've got no direct connections to police or county officials."

"One of those fine citizens will make a deal when you start applying pressure," KD said.

"Maybe."

"Where we going?" Blunt asked.

"Having you two around raises too many questions. Your warrantless searches could muddy our case. We'll keep the car and gear you picked up at Midwest Sporting Goods. Check out of the Holiday Inn Express and go to the Des Moines airport."

"Sure you don't want our help?" KD asked.

"It's all FBI from here on out."

Twenty minutes later, Martinez pulled up in front of the entry to the Holiday Inn Express. He grabbed a set of car keys from the console. "These go to the blue Prius parked next to the building. Leave it at the Enterprise car rental at the airport. Your airline tickets are in the glove box."

KD AND BLUNT stopped by the front desk to get fresh keycards and then took the elevator up to their rooms.

"So we're all done here," Blunt said.

"We don't work for the FBI," KD said.

"Yeah, but Garcia had us helping them, and they don't want our help anymore."

"Garcia had us looking into a conspiracy."

"What's on your mind, Doc?"

"Did Martinez want to get rid of us because he's concerned about his case or because he doesn't want us to interfere with his cover-up?"

"Who's he covering up for?"

"Don't know. Crooked FBI agents? Granger's connections? The bad press they're going to get if they go to court?"

"Maybe he just doesn't want to have to explain all the laws we broke to the US Attorney."

"Maybe," KD said. "You with me or you going home?"

"I'm not leaving without you, Doc. What's your plan?"

"We know the sheriff is dirty. Let's keep an eye on him. The drug business is in turmoil. What's he going to do?"

"You going to clear this with Garcia?"

"When we find something."

"FBI won't like it."

"They're going to be too busy to notice us. At least for a while. We'll check out of here, switch cars, find another motel."

. . .

GRANGER HOLLERED to his wife over his shoulder. "Go stay with your sister." He ran down the steps from his house with a duffel containing some clothes, a laptop computer, and $50,000 cash. The FBI wouldn't arrest his wife—she was completely innocent—although they'd probably make a mess searching the house. Gomez opened the back seat passenger's door of the Suburban for him and shut it after he got in. Granger looked up at Smits in the driver's seat. "Get going."

"Where to?"

"The house we bought under your ex-wife's name."

Smits took off, Gomez following in a Cadillac Escalade.

"How many guys do we have left?" Granger asked.

"I don't know, Henry. We lost the guys at the warehouses. And we aren't going to be able to use the R&G trucks. Maybe it's time to run."

"I'm not giving up what we've built. Not yet. As long as we can keep our pipeline open, we'll be able to stay in business."

"The Mexicans are going to be pissed."

"They'll get over it. We just might have to go back and forth to Mexico ourselves."

"That's more danger than we're used to."

"That's what starting over looks like. We've got to move fast. And we've got to keep the money flowing. But first things first. We've got to stay ahead of the FBI, and we've got to hire some new help."

TEN MINUTES LATER, an FBI strike team wearing tactical gear squealed up in front of Granger's house and kicked down the front door. His wife was standing in the kitchen in her bathrobe. "What the hell do you think you're doing?"

Agent Ables handed her the search warrant. "We're searching your house. You'll have to wait on the porch."

Granger's lawyer hustled up onto the porch thirty minutes later, her hair still wet from the shower. "Don't say anything."

· · ·

TWO HOURS LATER, Jimmy and Roslyn were sitting in a conference room at the courthouse across a table from Agent Ables, who'd changed out of tactical gear and into a black pantsuit. A recorder sat on the table between them.

"So Mateo Smits and Rudy Gomez came to Roslyn's mother's house and picked you up?"

"Yes," Roslyn replied.

"Said Mr. Granger needed to see you immediately?"

"More or less," Jimmy said.

"Didn't that seem strange?"

"Yeah, but Mr. Granger always had to have his way. So not that strange for him."

"And why did you call your father?"

"Because I guess I thought it was just a little too weird."

"And your father said?"

"He'd take care of it."

"Meaning?"

"He'd talk to Mr. Granger."

"And they took you out to the warehouse in the country and kept you in the room where we found you?"

"Yes," Roslyn replied. "Rudy Gomez brought us food. We didn't see anyone else."

"Not even Mr. Granger?"

They both said no.

Ables turned to Jimmy. "Did you ever call to your father while you were at the warehouse?"

"They took our phones."

"Didn't you think it was strange that your father couldn't get you released?"

"Yes, I did. I didn't know what to make of it. I assumed he was trying to get leverage on Mr. Granger."

"What kind of leverage?"

"I don't know."

"Can you think of anything else?"

Jimmy Crowder rubbed his chin. "So Mr. Granger, Mateo, and Rudy were all involved in some sort of organized crime?"

"That's what the evidence suggests."

"Were they the ones that killed our friends?" Roslyn asked.

"We don't know yet," Ables replied.

"But you haven't arrested any of them?"

"We'll have them in custody soon enough. In the meantime, you're not in any danger, Ms. Billings."

"Okay."

Ables glanced from one to the other. "Nothing else? I'll have an agent take you home."

The FBI agent dropped them off in front of the Billings house. Jimmy Crowder turned to walk up the sidewalk to the porch, but Roslyn didn't move. She stood on the sidewalk in front of the house, looking at Jimmy as if she wasn't sure she knew him.

"You knew they were criminals."

"Yes, I did."

"Did you do anything wrong?"

"I let them use me to do wrong."

"Your job?"

He nodded.

"Did your father know?"

"It's complicated."

"Did you know they killed Pat and Susan, Mike, Billy, and Philip?"

"I suspected they had. I was pushing Dad to investigate, helping the NDA agents, but I didn't know for a fact. I'm telling you the truth. I wasn't involved that way, and if I had been, I would have tried to stop them. They were my friends, for Christ's sake."

She stepped up to him, placed her hand on his chest, and looked up into his eyes. "Okay," she said. "I believe you. But from here on out, no secrets."

"No secrets."

"I've got one more question for you. Are we leaving together or am I leaving alone? Because I can't live in Mercy Creek anymore."

He put his hands on her hips. "We're leaving together, babe. We're getting out of here, and we're never coming back."

LATER THAT AFTERNOON, Ables and Martinez sat in the living room at the farmhouse, where Martinez had set up his office.

"Granger's house was clean," Ables said. "The men and women taken at the hidden warehouse in the country aren't R&G employees, and the property's owned by a dummy corporation, although the semitrucks were R&G trucks. Jimmy Crowder and Ms. Billings never left the room at the warehouse and only saw Smits and Gomez. We didn't find anything incriminating at the main R&G warehouses in town, although drugs and a drug lab were found at the Comanche Pass warehouse and guns were found in a semitruck parked at the Eagle Grove warehouse. Two of R&G's Mercy Creek employees have already implicated Smits and Gomez. We're taking their statements now. That's all of it."

"It's a good first day," Martinez replied. "We just need to keep pushing with our interrogations."

"What about Sheriff Crowder?"

"After what his son and the girlfriend said? Let's put him under surveillance."

10

The next day, KD and Blunt sat in a beat-up pickup truck on the town square, watching Ables and Michaels in one of their surveillance cars in the corner of a strip mall parking lot watching the front of the county jail. Sheriff's deputies' cruisers came and left at shift changeover. Sheriff Crowder went to lunch, met with a county supervisor at an administrative building, went home at 5:30 p.m., and stayed in all evening.

The next morning, while the sheriff was driving to work, a plumber's van two cars ahead of him ran a red light. He turned on his lights and siren and pulled them over. Ables drove by and turned right at the next intersection, but Blunt, who was farther behind, had time to pull into a parking lot across the street. KD got out her binoculars and watched the sheriff talking with a blocky, mustached guy. She passed the binoculars to Blunt. "You know him?"

"It's one of Granger's guys," he said.

"You sure?"

"Yep. His fist left a bruise on my right cheek."

"I'd love to know what they're talking about."

"Think Ables knows who it is?"

"They'd be swarming the van if they knew."

After the sheriff gave the driver his ticket and his driver's license and registration back, the van pulled back into traffic.

"Follow the van."

Blunt followed the van down Johnson Boulevard onto Roosevelt Street and out of town on a county road. The van turned down a gravel drive. Blunt pulled off the road where the ditch was shallow and rolled behind a clump of scraggly cedar trees.

"Okay," KD said. "Let's see what we've got."

They climbed the cow fence and walked through the tall grass in the pasture back toward the gravel drive. After a few minutes, they could see a barn surrounded by sycamore trees up on the hill. "The van's coming back down," Blunt said.

They lay flat in the grass until the van had turned back onto the county road.

"Maybe one of us should have stayed with the truck," Blunt said.

"Maybe," KD replied. "Too late now."

They continued up to the barn. No surveillance cameras, no one on guard on this side, no one looking out from the hay loft door. They crept along the wall until they found a missing knot hole. KD peeked in. Four men and two women, sitting on old sofas and recliners, playing games on their phones or chatting. KD motioned to Blunt. He peeked through the hole, and then he put his lips up to KD's ear. "No Granger."

She nodded.

They crept around the side of the barn to get a look at the other side. A black Jeep and a Ford F-150 were parked on the grass. They slipped back down the hill. When they were out of hearing range, Blunt said, "Sorry looking crew. I recognized the guy with the mustache and one other guy."

"Granger must be somewhere else."

"He could have been the one driving the van away."

"I don't think so. Security was pretty lax there. Not even one person on lookout."

"Must be pretty sure they won't be found."

"Or pretty stupid. Wonder how many of these cells they have?"

"Hope it's the only one."

"That would make it easier for us," KD said. "We need another car, just in case they decide to change hideouts."

"One to follow and one to surveil."

"Exactly."

They drove back into town to the Enterprise Rent-A-Car. KD dropped Blunt off and went back out to the barn. She parked off the road behind a fat maple where she could look up the hill through the branches and see the barn. Blunt rented a white Sentra. Then he drove to a Casey's General Store and bought snacks and drinks before he drove back out to the barn. When he got there, he parked behind KD and got into the truck with her.

"I went up for a look," KD said. "They're all still there, as well as the Jeep and the truck."

They sat and waited. At 3:15 p.m., the Jeep came down the driveway. Blunt followed in the Sentra, staying well back until they were in city traffic on Elm Street. When the Jeep pulled into the drive through of a KFC, Blunt parked in a space at the Taco John's across the street. He called KD.

"Food run. The Jeep's at the KFC."

"The van came back a minute ago. If it leaves, I'm going to follow."

The Jeep turned left back onto Elm Street, going back the way it came. Blunt gave it plenty of room. It was disappearing behind the barn when he reached the bottom of the driveway. KD was gone. He got out his smartphone.

"Where are you, Doc?"

"Smits is driving the van," she replied. "We're on Jansen Road heading south, just west of town."

"Keep me up to speed."

"You bet."

The van pulled into a run-down, two-pump gas station at a crossroads. KD turned right at the corner and then made a U-turn when she was hidden from the van by the building. She pulled off behind the gas station and got out of the truck. She stood beside an old Mr. Igloo ice freezer and watched Smits pump gas into the van and wash the windshield before he went into the building. He came out a few minutes later with a bottle of Coke in his hand. She ran back to the truck. When Smits drove through the crossroads, KD followed, keeping her distance.

At the next crossroads, Smits turned left onto the gravel road. KD followed behind the cloud of dust. The sun was low in the sky to her right, the night coming on, the trees along the ditches turning into silhouettes. Smits turned on his headlights. KD kept driving in the dark, using the van's taillights to mark her way. Finally, the van pulled into the yard of a two-story farmhouse located next to a lightning-blasted tree. There were no lights shining from the house and no vehicles in the yard. Smits turned off his headlights and got out of the van.

KD pulled over on the side of the road next to a harvested corn-field. She turned off the interior light before she got out of the truck and eased the door closed. She moved quietly across the field of clotted dirt and corn stubble, listening as hard as she could, her hand on the gun in her jacket pocket. No one was in the front yard near the van, no one was in the side yard, but around behind the house, she saw a crack of light coming from under the side door to a barn. She crept toward the barn, taking care not to stumble in the dark, until she was finally close enough to hear voices.

"It's tricky, Henry," Smits said. "The FBI is all over everything, so we can't use any of the properties listed to shell corporations or even dead people. But I've got Rudy working on a widow. We're setting her up with a condo in Florida for the winter. We'll be able to use her place off the books. It's perfect. A little acreage, no near neighbors. Three or four more days max, and you're back to creature comforts."

"Heard from our people?"

"They've all been moved to the Polk County Jail."

"Fucking FBI. How's morale?"

"Our second-string guys are all whining. Might have to make an example of a few of them to get the others to step up."

"You know what's best."

"I'll be back tomorrow with everything on your shopping list."

"Thanks."

KD slipped around the side of the barn and watched Smits come out of the barn and walk back toward the farmhouse. Then she heard the van start and saw the headlights disappear down the road.

She hurried off across the harvested field, moving faster as she got out of earshot, the clods of dirt crunching under her shoes. When she was back in the truck, she called Blunt. "Found Granger."

"You sure?"

"Overheard him and Smits talking. Smits left in the van. Might be coming back to you, I don't know."

"Should I come to you?"

"No need. Granger will definitely be here tomorrow. Let's meet back at the motel."

They parked side by side around the back of the Days Inn away from the pole lights and walked around to the front entry. The parking lot was about three-quarters full. The receptionist looked up from his computer, but he didn't say anything. They got in the elevator.

"Surprised we found him so quickly," KD said.

"You shake enough bushes; the rats start running. You ready to call the boss?"

"Definitely."

They went into KD's room. KD made an encrypted call to Garcia's personal smartphone and put it on speaker.

"This better be good," Garcia said.

KD filled her in on what they'd done since the FBI arrived.

"So the FBI told you to leave, and you've been working behind their backs?"

"Yes."

"I haven't heard anything about this."

Blunt cut in. "No *atta-boy* from Special Agent-in-Charge Victor?"

Garcia ignored him. "So the sheriff led you to Granger and now you want to put Granger under surveillance in hopes of obtaining evidence of an ongoing conspiracy involving government officials?"

"That's exactly what we want to do, boss," KD replied.

"Why don't you go to the FBI? Let them obtain the correct warrants?"

"Because I don't trust them. They still might be compromised."

"I know Victor. He squeaks when he walks. There's no way he's involved in anything illegal."

"But he's not here. Thus far, all the FBI has done is roll up the drug crews. No law enforcement or government officials have been implicated."

"These things can take time."

"Maybe."

Garcia sighed. "Okay. I'll go to the FISA court first thing in the morning. Tina will send someone with the gear you'll need."

"Assault gear and the surveillance tech?" Blunt asked.

"Everything."

"Thanks, boss," KD replied.

"Don't screw this up. Stay off the FBI's radar. I don't want to have to explain anything to Victor unless you have the evidence."

EARLY THE NEXT MORNING, KD and Blunt were sitting at the square table in KD's motel room, eating take-out breakfast from a truck stop diner.

"Okay," KD said, "let's talk this through."

Blunt shoved a forkful of pancakes into his mouth and washed it down with coffee. "Someone's got to be on Granger all the time."

"Agreed. Once we set the tech, it's six hours on, six hours off, until we have the evidence or have to take him." She cut up her over-easy eggs and dipped her toast into the yolk.

"From the GPS map, it looks like we're lying in the farm field or hiding in the house or on the other side of the road in the culvert under the field access driveway."

"They've all got their problems. Out in the farm field, it's a standard camouflage situation, unless someone gets too close."

"Hiding in the house offers the best proximity. But getting in and out would be difficult."

"The culvert provides more cover and chance of escape, but if it rains—"

"Still the best place to start from."

"Then that's it," KD said.

"The courier will be here with our gear by 5:00 p.m."

"In the meantime, we need to scout the location for the best place to set the surveillance equipment."

"And we need to make sure Granger doesn't change location," Blunt said. "Wish we had a Stingray device to tap his cell phone."

"We'd have to drive one across the country. Couldn't borrow one from the Feds out of Chicago or Kansas City without showing our hand."

After breakfast, they drove the pickup truck back out to the farm where Granger was hiding. In daylight, the farmhouse and the barn seemed more exposed. The harvested cornfield and the blasted tree in front of the house offered no cover. At the same time, anyone on the property had an uninterrupted sightline in all directions. They drove by without slowing down.

"Can't just park on the road," Blunt said. "No way to get to the culvert without being seen."

"In this part of the country, all the roads are on a grid. Maybe the road to the south is close enough." She took a right at the first intersection, and then another right onto a narrow gravel road at the next intersection.

"This road is just for moving farm equipment," Blunt said. He kept looking north as she drove. "There it is. Pull over."

KD pulled over at a low spot where they could only see the roof of the barn directly to their north.

"Good call, Doc. Let's go in from here."

They climbed the barbed wire fence and made their way through the corn stubble, moving quickly and quietly. There was no one in sight. Not a tractor, or a truck, or a person on foot. When they got to the back of the barn, they knelt in the unmown grass and listened, but they couldn't hear anything. KD glanced at Blunt. Had Granger changed his mind and left in the night? They moved along the side of the barn, stepping carefully, looking for any crack or gap where they might peek inside. As they were moving along the right side, they heard a screen door slam, and then footsteps. They crouched against the side of the barn. Someone was talking, his voice getting louder as he approached. It was Granger.

"Bring me some coffee. I ran out. And a breakfast burrito while you're at it." He paused. "No one's working these fields this morning. So there's no risk of being seen. Hurry up."

KD and Blunt trotted back across the field to their truck. "He's going to be here for a while," KD said. "I'll drive you back to the motel so you'll have the other vehicle. Then I'll drive back out here and take the first shift."

"I could just leave you here. Then there'd be no truck on the road."

"But what if he leaves? We need a vehicle here so that we can follow him."

After KD dropped off Blunt, she drove back to the same spot on the gravel road and made her way back across the field to the back of the barn. She could hear Granger talking, but she couldn't make out what he was saying. She looked out toward the road in front of the farmhouse. There weren't any vehicles in the driveway. Smits or whomever must have already delivered the food. She examined the vertical siding on the back of the barn. It was weather tight. There were a few small gaps between the bottom of the siding and the ground. Maybe they could worm a snake camera through one of them.

A tawny farm cat came out of the weeds along the edge of the field, strolled across the yard directly toward her, and sat down at her feet. KD tried to shoo the cat away without making any noise. The cat purred, rubbed up against her ankles, and sat back down, looking up at her as if expecting something. Granger was still talking. KD motioned with her foot. The cat yowled. KD sprang from her spot and took off for the farm field, where she hopped the fence and lay down behind the tall grass growing along the fence line.

Granger crept around the corner of the barn with a pistol in his hand, saw the cat and smiled. "Looking for food, kitty?" he asked. He bent down and scratched the cat behind the ears. "Come on, I've got something for you." The cat followed him.

KD lay in the field for another ten minutes before she crept back to the barn. Lucky break. The cat distracting him made her job easier. She slipped around to the left side of the barn and looked up at the opening to the hay loft. Was there a way to get up there? That would be the perfect place to set up an audiovisual recorder. She walked back out into the farm field, veering off to the left so that she had a clear view of anyone going to or from the barn, and sat down in the corn stubble to wait.

At 1:00 p.m., Blunt came to relieve her. She went through a McDonald's drive-through on her way back to the motel, ate, took a nap, and was drinking coffee when she got the call from the operative who was bringing their equipment. She drove down the interstate to the nearest rest stop. There were three semitrucks parked in the truck parking and a minivan and a beat-up Toyota Yaris parked in front of the entrance to the welcome center. She pulled in next to a blue Ford Escape parked on the far side of the building near the dog-walking area.

A young man wearing a suit and tie, sunglasses pushed back on his head, got out of the Escape when she climbed out of her truck. "Captain Thorne," he said.

"Let's see what you brought," she replied.

He raised the liftback to reveal three large plastic cases. KD lowered the tailgate on the truck. The man set the first case down on the tailgate. KD opened it just enough to see what was inside. Automatic rifle, pistol, magazines of ammunition fitted into impressions, body armor strapped into the lid. She shut the lid and slid the case into the bed of the truck. The man set the second case down. It was the same as the first. The third case contained two communications headsets and the surveillance gear. KD raised the tailgate. "Thanks. Give my regards to Agent Han."

KD sat in the truck and watched the Ford Escape drive away before she left the rest stop, drove up to the first interchange, and turned around. She drove back out to where Blunt had parked the Sentra in the low spot on the gravel road behind the barn. She texted him. *Got the gear. I'm at your car.*

He stood up in the field and jogged out to her.

"Anything happening?"

"All quiet. He's been on his phone, but no one's come out here. Every few hours, he sneaks into the house."

"Bathroom?"

"Who knows?" Blunt looked in the bed of the truck. "What have you got?"

KD opened the surveillance gear case. Blunt looked over the gear. "A snake camera, a minicamera microphone combo, camouflage sleeping bag and cover, comms sets, and night vision goggles." He held up the minicamera. "Tina came through. The visuals and sound off this model are excellent."

"So what do you think?"

"Slip the snake camera under the siding in hopes of capturing a visual."

She nodded. "And the minicam could go anywhere."

"Anywhere inside."

"I'd like to get up in the loft."

"Yeah, but I don't see how."

"It would be a great place to record from."

"You think anyone important is going to come here to meet him? This is a way station."

"But does he have another place to go to? We're hoping he has to use his contacts to make his escape."

"All true."

"Let's get set up."

They locked the gun cases inside the truck cab, put on their comms sets, and crept across the corn stubble in the fading light. A Suburban was now parked in the driveway, and they could hear talking coming from inside the barn. At the back wall, Blunt found a spot to slip the snake camera under the wall. They looked on the five-inch display screen. All they could see was darkness. They moved around to the right side of the barn and tried again. Now they could see the packed dirt floor and the legs of a folding table. Blunt turned the snake. They could see two men sitting at the folding table, but they couldn't make out who they were in the dim light. They turned on their comms to hear the audio from the snake.

"I'm still working on it, Henry," they heard Smits say. "It's not so easy. Thought I had a place ready to go, and the FBI raided it. So I'm hunting down another spot."

"What about that rental over on Sycamore Drive?" Granger asked.

"A car's been watching it."

"Christ."

"We can still run."

"I run, I lose the pipeline. Everything we built up. Right now, we've lost R&G, we'll have to set up a new front company, but we've still got all our connections and the people we've bought off."

"It might be easier to set up someplace new."

"You think Juarez is going to let us walk away? We know too much about his business. We've got to fight it out here. Is Rudy making any progress with the widow?"

"You've just got to be patient. It would be better if you went through one more temporary place before you landed at the acreage. We've got make sure the FBI can't track you. This barn may not be comfortable, but at least it's safe."

"How's my wife?"

"She hasn't been arrested. But she didn't go to her sister's. She's still living in the house. Good thing you never took any business home."

"And our guys?"

"Nobody's coming to work."

"Not even the R&G employees?"

"Not even them. I should get going. You need anything else?"

"No, I'll see you in the morning."

Blunt pushed the snake camera display down into the weeds before he and KD crept to the left back corner of the barn, where they watched Smits cross the yard to a Suburban and drive away.

Then they made their way back through the field, taking care not to stumble in the dark, until they were back at the truck and the white Sentra. KD unlocked the truck and gave Blunt one of the weapons cases. "See you in six."

Blunt drove away. KD went out in the field carrying the camouflage sleeping bag, a pair of night vision goggles, and her comms headset. She set up in a spot in the corn stubble where she could watch the barn and the road. She was close enough to hear the audio from the snake camera over her comms. She unrolled the sleeping bag, climbed in, rested her chin on her folded arms and settled in.

MARTINEZ AND ABLES sat in the living room of the farmhouse. "So the drug cases and the gun cases are made?"

"Yes, Chris," Ables replied. "At all the locations—here, Eagle Grove, and Comanche Pass."

"We've made a lot of arrests."

"Looked great on the six o'clock news."

"But no one is willing to implicate any law enforcement or government officials?"

"They roll on direct supervisors, but those supervisors are either still at large or aren't responding to our pressure."

"Multiple charges, enhanced prison time, long stays at the worst prisons?"

"Thus far, it doesn't make any difference. Since the deaths at the Polk County Jail, they're more afraid of their bosses than prison time."

"And our ongoing surveillances?"

"We're following the sheriff here, the sheriff of Eagle County, Oklahoma, and that Texas ranger out of Comanche Pass, but they're all just going about their business."

"They're going to trip up eventually."

"I hope so."

11

At about 1:30 a.m., Blunt drove out to the farm to relieve KD. She went back to the motel, set her alarm for 6:00 a.m., and went to bed. In the morning, she bought breakfast at a drive-through and got back to the farmhouse by 7:30 a.m. Nothing had happened in the night. Smits had left about thirty minutes earlier. They hadn't talked about anything actionable. Blunt left and KD crawled into the sleeping bag.

At 9:15 a.m. an old Ford Ranger truck came down the gravel road behind the barn and stopped behind KD's truck. She'd seen the dust cloud and heard the truck on the gravel. She tucked her gear inside the sleeping bag and crept back toward the truck, keeping low to the ground. A man wearing a barn coat and a seed company cap was walking around her truck, looking inside and trying the door. KD stood up and walked toward him.

"Hey."

The man turned. "Hey."

"What's up?"

"This your truck?"

"Yep."

"You're trespassing."

KD showed him her ID. "I'm a federal agent on official government business."

"What are you doing out here?"

"I can't say."

"Is it something to do with the FBI in town?"

"All I can tell you is that I'm involved in an ongoing investigation."

"I see."

"And I need your cooperation."

"All right."

"So please don't tell anyone that you've seen me."

"I can do that."

"Thank you. We'll get off your property just as soon as we can."

The man got in his truck and drove away. KD watched the dust settle in his wake. Did she need to move her truck? Maybe. If that farmer noticed it, someone else might. But she couldn't do it now. She needed to wait for Blunt, and it was too early to contact him. She crept back across the field to her sleeping bag and went back to her surveillance.

At about 12:45 p.m., KD saw a Jeep turn up the driveway to the farmhouse. As she was pulling her binoculars up to her face, she heard footfalls behind her. She rolled over, pulling her pistol. Smits and two other men were standing over her, one holding a shotgun and the other a machine pistol.

"Toss the gun real slow," Shotgun guy said.

She tossed the pistol into the corn stubble.

"Well, *chica*," Smits said, "The farmer wasn't lying. Word has it the FBI ran you off."

Machine Pistol guy picked up her gun.

"Get up out of the bag," Smits said.

KD crawled out of the sleeping bag. Machine Pistol guy grabbed her by the collar of her shirt, pulled her to her feet, and pushed her toward Shotgun guy.

Smits got out his phone and sent a text. Then he turned to Machine Pistol guy. "Bring it all."

Machine Pistol guy rolled her comms headset and binoculars into the sleeping bag. They led her across the field, Shotgun guy walking behind her with his shotgun pointed at her back. A Suburban was coming down the gravel road toward them.

"Where's your partner?" Smits asked.

"He got reassigned."

"As curious as I am, we're not going to make the same mistake we made last time."

The Suburban stopped in the road behind her truck. The liftback went up.

"Truck keys," Machine Pistol said.

She reached into her pants pocket and handed him the truck keys.

He handed the keys to Shotgun guy. Then he pushed her around so she faced the cargo space, zip-tied her hands behind her back, pushed her into the SUV, and zip-tied her ankles together.

Shotgun guy got into her truck. Smits got into the front seat passenger's side of the Suburban and Machine Pistol guy got in the back. Smits turned to the driver. "Let's go."

"What about her partner?" Machine Pistol guy asked.

"You know where he is or what he's doing? One asshole at a time. We're not splitting up," Smits replied.

BLUNT CALLED KD on his way out to the farm at 1:15 p.m. to see if she wanted him to bring anything, but the call rolled over to voice mail. When he turned onto the gravel road behind the barn, her truck was gone. He tried calling again. Still no answer. He parked in their usual place, snatched up his comms headset, and jogged across the field to where she should have been set up, but there was nothing there, just corn stubble and clotted earth. He looked across at the farmhouse and barn. No people, no cars. He put on his comms headset. Granger was talking on his phone. Where was KD?

He jogged back to his car and called her again. No answer. What to do? He could keep watching Granger. Stay on task. But something was wrong. KD wouldn't break protocol. The snake camera was recording whatever Granger was saying. As long as he couldn't leave the barn, they didn't need to watch him. What had Smits said? At least another day.

Blunt got out his smartphone and called Tina.

"What's up, Blunt?"

"Can you find KD's phone?"

"Hold on."

A few minutes later she came back on. "The phone is in Evergreen State Park. It's to the southwest of you. I'm texting the map and the exact GPS coordinates."

"Thanks."

"Do you need backup? Should I contact the FBI?"

"Need to keep them out of the loop. I'll let you know if I need anything else."

Blunt drove the county road south, following the route laid in on his smartphone, until he went through the gate of Evergreen State Park and pulled into the first parking lot. There were no cars there. He popped the trunk and opened his weapons case. He took off his jacket, put on the Kevlar vest, and put his jacket back on. He picked up the AR-15 rifle, slid a full magazine into place, and put two spare magazines into his pockets. His SIG Sauer pistol was holstered at his hip. He tapped his back pocket to make sure his lockback knife was there. Then he looked at the GPS map on his phone again. KD was on the other side of the ridge to the west of his current location, on a narrow trail off a side road past a picnic table. Maybe she was dead, or maybe he was running straight into trouble. Either way, there was no time to lose. He took off up the hill at a run, the hyperawareness kicking in, his mind going to that quiet place where the killing came from.

At the top of the ridge, he moved at a crouch until he found cover behind a small spruce. Down below, he could see the Suburban and KD's truck, and he could hear distant voices. He slipped down the other side of the ridge, cradling the AR-15, and then wormed his way through the brush until he was squatting behind the Suburban. A man stood between the vehicles, watching something further down the hill. Blunt slipped around to the front bumper of the Suburban.

KD was standing waist deep in a hole, digging, the earth piled up on the other side of her. Smits and two guys he hadn't seen before were standing over her, casually chatting. Smits had his hands in his jacket pockets. One of the men held a shotgun, the other a machine pistol.

Blunt moved silently back around the Suburban. He laid his rifle down and pulled out his lockback knife. A bird called off in the distance, the shovel bit into the earth, the men chatted. Blunt sprang up, made two steps, slapped his free hand over the man's mouth, and plunged the knife through the man's throat as he pulled him to the ground. He listened. The men were still chatting. He wiped the knife on the man's leg, put it back in his pocket, and picked up his rifle.

Blunt slipped around to the left, moving silently through the brush, until he'd worked his way around to the other side of KD, who was still digging. Now came the tricky part. Shotgun guy was pointing right at KD. If he shot him first, the shotgun might go off and kill her. Machine Pistol guy was pointing his gun at the ground. And he had to assume that Smits had a gun in his pocket. A lot depended on what KD did when all hell broke loose.

Just as KD flipped another shovel of dirt out of the hole, Blunt fired a short burst. Machine pistol guy went down. Shotgun guy swung his weapon around and Smits pulled a pistol from his pocket. KD disappeared into the hole. Blunt zigzagged in, firing as he came. A shotgun blast missed to his right. Shotgun guy went down. Smits fired wild. One round hit Blunt in the vest, knocking him backward. He pulled his SIG Sauer and tossed it into the hole to KD. Smits was running toward the Suburban, firing over his shoulder, yelling for the dead guy to start the SUV. Blunt flipped over onto his stomach, held his breath, then sighted Smits with his rifle.

"Don't kill him," KD said.

He glanced toward the hole. KD fired the SIG Sauer and Smits went down. She scrambled out of the hole and ran toward him, Blunt on her heels. Smits was trying to crawl away, blood seeping from his right leg.

"You don't want to die," KD said.

Smits tossed his pistol away.

She knelt beside him. After she zip-tied his wrists behind his back, she examined the wound to his thigh. "Through and through. Not bleeding too much. Looks like I missed the artery." She looked up at Blunt. "Wasn't sure you'd find me."

"Tina tracked your phone."

She smiled. "Managed to keep it this time. I hid it in the back of the Suburban. It was the only thing I could think of. That was a hard shot into your vest. You moving okay?"

He nodded. "How about you?"

"Feeling a lot better now. Why don't you get the first aid kit out of the truck?"

KD dressed Smits's wound, while Blunt checked the others. "Any of them need medical attention?" KD asked.

Blunt shook his head.

Smits looked from KD to Blunt. "We can still make a deal."

"Think so?" KD replied.

"Suitcases of money. Not small bills either. The FBI can't find them. Only me and Henry know about them."

"What makes you think we want money?" Blunt asked.

"Everyone wants money. Money and recognition. I'll tell you whatever you want to know about Henry's operation, and I'll tell you where the money is."

"What do you think, Doc?"

"Let's put him in the Suburban."

Blunt grabbed Smits by the shoulder and helped him to his feet. Then he walked him to the back of the Suburban. KD climbed into the cargo area and got her smartphone out of the crevice she'd pushed it down into. After she climbed out, Blunt helped Smits into the cargo area and zip-tied his ankles together.

KD and Blunt walked out of earshot.

"Smits is not going to give us his full cooperation," Blunt said. "He'll shine us on first chance he gets."

"I know. But this situation might work to our advantage. If we take Smits and the rest of his crew off the board, that could make life a lot more difficult for Granger."

"Time to involve the FBI?"

She shook her head. "We're not bringing them into this until we can prove the corruption."

"Then what do you want to do?"

"We know Sheriff Crowder is corrupt, so let's give Smits to the sheriff. If he arrests him, Granger will have to reach out to someone else. And if he doesn't arrest him, we'll have evidence to use against the sheriff."

"I like the way you think, Doc."

KD got out her phone, called Tina, and put the phone on speaker. "Are you still tapped into the Sheriff's Department's phones and computers?"

"Affirmative."

She turned to Blunt. "We're good to go."

She put away her phone and found a phone in the pants pocket of the man who'd been standing with the vehicles. She called the county jail. "Mateo Smits is trussed up in the back of a Suburban out in Evergreen State Park. He's got a leg wound. Three of his guys are dead."

She ended the call and tossed the phone onto the man's body. "Let's get back to our stake out."

AN HOUR LATER, Sheriff Crowder parked behind the Suburban in Evergreen State Park. He got out of his Ford Explorer, noticed the dead man lying beside the Suburban, and glanced down the hill at the open grave and the two men lying beside it, before he went back to the Suburban and raised the liftback.

Smits was lying on his side, his head angled onto the mat. "About time you got here."

"You've got a fucking mess here, Mateo."

"Cut me loose, bury these guys, and let's get out of here."

The sheriff put one foot up on the bumper of the Suburban. "I got a call at the jail that you were out here."

"So?"

"So what if the FBI is testing me?"

"You're just being paranoid. If they suspected anything, you'd already be indicted. Look around. It doesn't get any easier than this. The hole is already dug."

"Sorry, Mateo, I just can't do it."

"I go down, you go down."

"You don't know what I've done or haven't done. Maybe Henry told you this or that, but that's just hearsay."

"We'll see."

"Yes, we will."

The sheriff took out his smartphone. "Agent Martinez? This is Sheriff Crowder. I've found Mateo Smits."

"How?"

"Anonymous tip. Looks like he was in a gunfight. You want to secure the scene?"

"I'll get a team out there immediately. What's your location?"

AFTER AGENT MARTINEZ ended his call with the sheriff, he called Agent Ables. "Are you on the sheriff?"

"Yeah."

"Where are you?"

"Evergreen State Park. He's standing next to a Suburban."

"He just called me. Mateo Smits is in that Suburban. Stand by. I'm sending a team."

THAT EVENING, back at the farm, Blunt was back at their surveillance spot in the corn stubble, watching the barn and the area between the barn and the house through his night vision goggles. No vehicles were parked in the driveway, and the house was dark inside. Over his comms headset, he could hear Granger moving around in the barn. He was talking on his phone, but he was too far from the snake camera for Blunt to make out what he was saying.

Blunt shifted his weight. They had to find a way to deploy the minicam. There was no way they were going to get it up into the hayloft. The next time Granger left the barn for even a few minutes, he was going to try to find a place to install it.

Granger's voice was getting louder. "He and his guys were supposed to deal with a problem. He hasn't gotten back to me. Maybe I need to run." He paused. "Okay, you stop by. No lights after you turn onto the gravel. Come right now."

A few moments later, Granger come out of the barn, cut across the yard, and went into the back of the house, a flashlight lighting the ground in front of him.

Blunt scrambled across the field with his tech bag over his shoulder. He moved around to the side of the barn where he could see the back of the house. Then he felt the siding for a vertical row of nail heads, judged the width of the framing, and drilled a small hole through the siding next to the post. He looked at the back of the house. He could see the flashlight beam through an upstairs window. He took the minicam, pushed it in the hole, and then stuck some mud-colored putty over it. He paired the camera with his phone. The wide-angle image captured most of the room.

A car was rolling down the gravel road, its headlights off. Blunt scurried around behind the barn. He looked down at his phone screen and paired his comms set with the phone. Granger came back into the barn carrying a grocery bag, which he set on the folding table. A minute later Rudy Gomez came into the barn.

"So what have you heard?" Granger asked. "There's still nothing on the news."

"We've got nothing. Our girl in the sheriff's office hasn't heard a thing," Gomez replied.

Blunt smiled. The visual and the audio were crisp and clear.

Granger continued. "And Mateo?"

"Not a word."

"We've got to assume the worst." He handed Gomez the grocery bag. "Here's enough cash to get things set up."

"I'll take care of it."

"Don't fuck this up. That widow needs to move to Florida. Call me as soon as I can move to the acreage."

Blunt scurried back across the field to his car and drove east on the gravel road without turning on his headlights. He knew Gomez was one road farther north doing exactly the same thing. When he came to the intersection with Jansen Road, he pulled over. A few minutes later, he saw Gomez turn on his headlights and head north toward town. Blunt pulled out after him. Then he called KD and filled her in.

"So this is Granger's last hidey-hole," she said. "Call the sheriff."

Blunt input the sheriff's private phone number.

"Who is this?"

"I'm following Rudy Gomez on Jansen Road, headed north toward town."

"Why don't you tell the FBI?"

"Because I'm telling you."

"What's he driving?"

"Blue Nissan Pathfinder. Iowa plate number DFR592. Just passed Lincoln Drive."

"Okay." The sheriff ended the call.

Blunt kept following Gomez into town. A few minutes later, a sheriff's deputy's cruiser slid around the corner, flipped on its red and blue lights, and tapped its siren for Gomez's Nissan to pull over. The Nissan sped up. The cruiser took chase. Blunt slowed down, turned around in a Dunkin Donuts parking lot, and drove back out to the barn. He called KD.

"So Granger's main guys are off the table," KD said.

"He's all alone."

"So will he pay someone to bring him a car, or will he move up the food chain?"

"Tomorrow or the next day we'll know."

Blunt got out of his car and crossed the corn stubble to the back of the barn. He looked at his phone. The minicam was working perfectly. No need for the snake camera anymore. He slipped the snake camera out from under the barn siding, turned it off, and carried it back to his surveillance spot in the field.

MIDMORNING THE NEXT DAY, Agent Martinez walked down the hallway from Mateo Smits's and Rudy Gomez's cells at the county jail. They weren't talking yet, but they would be. They were all out of options. All their subordinates had flipped. They could carry all the weight of the drug trafficking and gun running, or they could cooperate and turn on Granger.

He walked down the hall to the sheriff's office and knocked on the open door. The sheriff looked up from his computer. "Come on in, Agent Martinez."

Martinez sat in the office chair across the desk from the sheriff.

"Coffee?"

"No thanks, Sheriff. I just dropped by to thank you for your help yesterday. I've got to admit that I was surprised. You seemed to know nothing about this criminal enterprise, and yet, now, here we are."

"Got lucky, I guess. Rooting out these drug dealers will make a big difference in our community. Wish I'd realized what was going on sooner. Those five kids murdered—it's a terrible tragedy, but at least they didn't die for nothing."

Martinez stood up. "Well, thanks again."

"I guess you're about done here."

"We're still hunting down Granger, but it shouldn't take much longer."

"What makes you think he's still here?"

"His two key lieutenants were still here yesterday, still actively committing crimes, so I'm guessing he's close by."

·   ·   ·

THAT AFTERNOON, the sheriff and his son stood in the driveway of the sheriff's house, standing at the back of a U-Haul truck. The ramp was down, and the back was about one-third filled with boxes.

"I see your mom gave you the bed out of the guest room," the sheriff said.

"It's a queen. The bed in my room is only a full."

"I can't talk you out of doing this?"

"Roslyn and I have been planning this for a long time. Just kept putting it off. Always needed just a little more money first. Were a little bit afraid to leave our friends. But when Granger's guys were holding us out at that warehouse, we just knew we had to go. And now, no job, no friends, nothing to hold us back."

"There's your mom."

"Des Moines isn't that far."

"Henry's gone now. He won't be able to come back. So you got your justice. I know the murders were a big shock, but we want you to stay here. You could go to the police academy, become a deputy."

"That's not for me, Dad."

"Think it over. If you change your mind, I'll hold the opening for a month."

"I appreciate the gesture, Dad, but I'm not going to change my mind. It's not just about me. It's what Roslyn wants, too."

TWO DAYS LATER, the sheriff, dressed in civilian clothes, drove a Dodge truck down the gravel driveway leading to a red barn behind an abandoned, two-story farmhouse. He parked around the back, away from the road, and went into the barn through the side door. A sleeping bag lay on a camping cot next to a reading lamp, and a laptop computer sat on a folding table. Granger stood, half hidden behind a ten-inch post, a pistol in his hand.

"Sheriff," Granger said as he stepped out into the room, "glad to see you."

The sheriff glanced around. "Pretty sad."

"That's why I need to move."

"Where are Mateo and Rudy?"

"If you don't know, they must have run," Granger replied.

The sheriff nodded his head. "After three of your guys were murdered in the Polk County Jail, I can't say I much blame them. I guess your Mexican partners are wanting your head. Do they know about this place?"

"Nobody knows about this place. Don't worry, my friend, I still have plenty of money to pay you."

"You kidnapped my boy."

"He was never at risk."

"Even if I didn't cooperate?"

"You were always going to cooperate."

"You're right about that."

The sheriff pulled a Glock from his jacket pocket. Granger raised his pistol, but he was too slow. The sheriff shot him twice in the chest, watched him crumple to the ground, and then stepped up to him and shot him in the head. He glanced around, wiped off the Glock with his handkerchief, and set it on the counter by the sink. He took out a burner phone.

"It's done."

"Can you deal with Smits and Gomez?"

"It's too late for that. FBI already has them."

"Fair enough. When we're ready to send the new guy, we'll be in touch."

The sheriff put on latex gloves and searched the room. In a cardboard box on the floor under some wooden shelves, he found Granger's duffel, which was half full of banded bundles of cash. He picked up the duffel, added the laptop from the folding table, and left.

KD FINISHED RECORDING the sheriff from the minicam in the wall of the barn and uploaded the footage to the cloud. She could hear Tina Han in her comms.

"Looks good. I'm sending a copy of this, along with your preliminary report, to Special Agent-in-Charge Jerome Victor at the Counter Terrorist Taskforce."

KD waited for the sheriff to drive away before she crawled out of the sleeping bag at her surveillance spot in the corn stubble. She crossed to the barn and went inside. Granger was definitely dead. She pried the minicam out of the wall of the barn, crossed back across the field to the sleeping bag, rolled her gear inside, and carried it all back to her pickup truck. Then she took out her phone and called Blunt. "I'm coming back to the motel. Granger is dead and we've got the goods on Sheriff Crowder."

"I was just looking at the video," Blunt said. "Impressive."

"You did a great job placing the minicam," she replied. "The assistant US attorney is going to love it."

THREE HOURS LATER, Agent Martinez and his team, in tactical gear and carrying assault rifles, rolled up in front of Sheriff Crowder's house in two Ford Explorers. Agent Ables took two agents around to the back. Martinez and three agents ran up the steps onto the porch. Martinez banged on the door. "Federal agents."

Sheriff Crowder opened the door. "What's this all about?"

"Sheriff Crowder," Martinez said, "you're under arrest for the murder of Henry Granger."

The agents swarmed him, cuffed his hands behind his back, and hustled him down to the second Explorer. They found the sheriff's wife standing in the kitchen, a spilled cup of coffee on the table beside her. "Who are you?"

"FBI, ma'am," Martinez said, "we have a warrant to search this house."

"This is absurd."

"You'll have to wait on the porch until we're done." One of the agents led her out of the kitchen.

The agents moved systematically through the house, searching every room, every closet, every cabinet, looking for any telltale sign of secret doors or hidden compartments. In the basement, under a rolling tool chest, two agents found a door cut into the floor. Inside the compartment, they found a sawed-off shotgun, a Colt revolver, and a duffel matching the description of the duffel from the barn. Inside were banded bundles of cash and a laptop computer. They brought the duffel and the guns to Martinez in the living room.

Martinez walked out onto the porch, where the sheriff's wife was sitting on the swing. "Ma'am, you're going to have to stay somewhere else tonight."

"Stay somewhere else? Well, I guess I need my things."

"Yes, ma'am. Agent Ables will escort you while you pack a bag."

THE NEXT MORNING, Sheriff Crowder, wearing an orange jumpsuit, sat in an interview room at the Teague County Jail. His right wrist was handcuffed to the ring on the table. Agent Martinez sat across from him. Martinez pushed a cup of coffee toward him. "I believe you take it black."

The sheriff reached for the cup. "Thanks."

"Bet you never expected to spend a night in one of your own cells."

The sheriff sipped his coffee.

Martinez opened a laptop on the table, opened the surveillance footage from the barn, turned the laptop toward the sheriff, and pressed play.

The sheriff nodded his head.

"And we found the duffel, the money, and Granger's laptop at your house."

"I expected as much."

"You're going to tell us everything you know if you want to avoid the death penalty."

The sheriff took another sip of coffee. "Witness protection. For me, my wife, my son, and his girlfriend."

"You don't have anything to bargain with. We've got you dead to rights."

"Three of Granger's men have already died in custody. And they were down at the Polk County Jail, not here. How many more will die before anyone goes to trial? No, I'm not taking chances. I don't help you, you say I'll get lethal injection. I help you, I'll be murdered in jail. On that basis, I've got no incentive to do anything. And you're going to want to know what I know. 'Cause I know everything."

"What exactly does that mean?"

"I know who the real bosses are."

"You're going to have to give us more than that if you want us to consider your proposition."

"Lawyer and witness protection."

"Do you have your own lawyer, or do you need a public defender?"

"Public defender will do for now."

"Then we'll talk again later."

"I want to see my wife."

"I'll see what I can arrange."

Martinez walked down the hallway to the sheriff's office, where KD and Blunt were waiting, and sat down behind the sheriff's desk.

"Enjoying your day thus far?" Blunt asked.

"I guess I should thank you for sticking around," Martinez said.

"Just wanted to finish the job," KD replied.

"You didn't trust me at all."

"Wasn't about trusting you. When we were sent here, we were told you guys couldn't take care of this yourself because you had a leak."

"But you're really done here now?"

"Yes, we're really done."

"You wouldn't know anything about the three dead guys we found out in Evergreen State Park?"

"Was it in our report?"

Martinez shook his head.

"Then I guess not," KD said. "What did Smits have to say?"

"He says he was unconscious. Doesn't know what happened."

"There you go." KD and Blunt stood up. "Don't want to miss our flight."

"Need a ride to Des Moines?"

"We're fine."

KD and Blunt walked out into the parking lot and got into the pickup truck. Blunt backed out of the parking space. "Well, the FBI will be eating on this case for a while. Feds, state, and locals fighting over who gets to confiscate what. Granger's crew rolled up from Texas all the way to Iowa. How long do you think it will stop the drugs and guns from flowing?"

"Not long enough. The cartel guys are probably already making new arrangements."

"Not our problem anymore."

"You're right about that."

Blunt turned onto Johnson Boulevard, heading toward the interstate. "What are you going to do when we get home?"

"Besides write the final report?"

"You had to bring that up."

"I'm going to take a bubble bath, get my nails done, go to the gym."

"You going to ask that guy on a date?"

"Maybe. What about you?"

"I'm going to eat some home cooking, sit in the Easy Boy, listen to my kids bicker and my wife shush them up."

"Domestic bliss."

"You got it."

12

Three days later, Sheriff Crowder and his son were facing each other across a table in an interview room at the Teague County Jail. "Really, Dad? Really?"

"Just plain bad luck."

"I can't believe you did it."

"He was the one who killed your friends."

"But you didn't kill him for that."

The sheriff couldn't meet his son's eyes. "You're right. But at least he was a bad guy. At least we won't have to pay the price."

"What are you talking about?"

"Witness protection. I'm making a deal with the FBI. I'm going to tell them everything I know, and then me and your mom and you and Roslyn will go into the WITSEC program."

Jimmy shook his head. "Roslyn won't agree to that. She wouldn't be able to see her mom anymore."

"If you don't go into the program, you won't last the year. The Mexicans are sure to kill you. And it won't be pretty."

"They won't care about us if we're not here or in the way."

"That's foolishness talking."

"Maybe, but we aren't really set up in Des Moines yet, so we can just go somewhere else."

"Talk to her. Maybe I can get her mom included."

"I'll tell her about it, but I think the answer is no."

A WEEK LATER, Martinez and Assistant US Attorney Benjamin were sitting in a conference room in the federal courthouse in Des Moines, Iowa. Sheriff Crowder and his attorney sat across the table. Crowder read the last page of his agreement with the government and turned to his attorney. "Seems fair."

"It's the best offer you're going to get," Martinez said.

"US marshals are standing by," Benjamin said. "You sign, your information proves out, and you're on your way."

"Hand me a pen," the sheriff said.

LATE THAT EVENING, in Washington, DC, KD locked the door to her apartment and kicked off her high heels. Civilian life was way too complicated. Her date had been disappointing. At the fitness studio, Toby was the guru of personal trainers. Everyone seemed to orbit around him, but in the restaurant, chatting, he seemed hesitant, unsure of himself. Not at all the guy she'd thought he would be.

She walked through to her bedroom, unzipped her dress and stepped out of it, and put the dress and her underwear in the laundry hamper. Maybe he'd been put off by the stitches under her eye. They were due to come out. But he could have said no when she'd asked him out. He'd seen her in workout clothes, seen the bruises and the scars.

She went into the bathroom and looked in the mirror. He had seemed surprised when she said she didn't drink. Didn't know him well enough to open that Pandora's box. And he couldn't quit talking about fitness and diet. Did he think he was out of his league when he found out she had a PhD, that she'd worked at NASA, that she couldn't talk about her work?

She brushed her teeth. He'd seemed so proud of his nephews and nieces. But most of what he talked about was work, sports, and TV. Thought her work must be like the shows he watched. She rinsed her mouth. She hadn't had a bad time, just not a good enough time that she wanted to sleep with him.

It was a shame. He would have been a monster in the sack, all that rippling muscle, all that knowledge about bodies, but that wasn't enough. Had to be able to talk about something in between, had to think there might the possibility of a relationship, but the spark just wasn't there.

She rubbed lotion on her arms and legs, took her nightgown off the hook behind the door, and pulled it on over her head. Would she go out with him again? Only if he asked. She hoped he wasn't going to get all weird about their one date. She'd hate to have to change gyms.

THREE WEEKS LATER, her ex-husband Frank was back in Washington, DC. This time they went out for dinner to a white-tablecloth tapas restaurant a few blocks from his hotel downtown.

"I missed you last month," Frank said. He sipped his red wine.

"Yeah, I was still out on that job."

"It turn out all right?"

"I've got a few new scars, but, yeah, it's all good."

"So it's you and Blunt, taking on all comers."

"Blunt's a great guy."

"I'm glad you've got the kind of partner who's got your back."

"Me, too." KD drank some sparkling water. "What about you? How's the NASA project going?"

"I like being the project leader. I don't like having to come up here to schmooze the suits every month."

She smiled. "If you didn't have to come up here, you wouldn't get to see me."

"I'd find some other reason."

Their server brought the first two small plates—grilled cauliflower in a spicy sauce and pieces of steak served on tiny flatbreads. Frank ordered another glass of wine and then took a large drink from the one he had.

"You okay?" KD asked.

"Just expecting bad news."

"From me?"

He nodded.

"You don't have to."

"I thought you were playing the field, dating other guys, making new friends."

"Sometimes I don't know what I want. Sometimes I think I'm just trying to find something to keep me busy."

"And you still don't think you can trust me?"

She shrugged. "You made your decisions. First to divorce me because I didn't want kids—if that was really the reason."

"It was."

"And then to decide you'd made a mistake and you wanted me back."

"I've always only loved you."

"But I'm the one who was rejected."

"I know."

"Made a fool of myself and wrecked my NASA career. Ended up drunk. So what happens if I let down my guard, take you back, and then you reject me again?"

"That's not going to happen."

"How would I feel then? I'd feel like I should have made sure I— this might seem hard—made my best decision. So that's what I'm doing."

"Okay."

"You may not like it, but that's where we are."

"I understand."

"You're still my guy, Frank. You're the only one besides Blunt that I can be completely honest with. So stop feeling sorry for yourself. It's unattractive."

"That's the pep talk?"

"That's all I've got." She drank some sparkling water. "Let's start eating before more plates show up."

TWO MONTHS LATER, Garcia called KD and Blunt into her office. "Have you read the file Tina put together on Mr. Juarez?"

They both nodded.

"Are we going to pick him up?" KD asked.

"He never leaves Mexico long enough for us to grab him in another country, and the Mexicans won't extradite him because it's a death penalty case. They've offered to arrest him, but that won't give us control of the interrogation. And the corruption up and down the I-35 corridor is a major embarrassment. Nobody wants that in the press. But we still need to know everything he knows about drug trafficking in the US."

"So it's a black bag job," Blunt said.

Garcia nodded. "Take him if you can, kill him if you can't. Tina has the details."

AT 3:00 A.M., KD and Blunt, wearing body armor and night vision goggles, were making their way down a rocky trail in the deep shadow in the bottom of an arroyo, Blunt in the lead. KD tapped her comms headset. "GPS map indicates we climb out after we make the next right turn."

Blunt grunted. "Wish we didn't have to use this obsolete gear."

"We can't use anything that the cartel's competition couldn't buy on the street."

"Infrared sighting wouldn't do any harm."

"Talk to the tech geeks when we get home."

"And don't even get me started on the RPG-7 launcher. I know everybody's got them, but the unguided targeting's unreliable."

"Yeah, the wind is going to be tricky, but we've got to have deniability if things go south. If the objective was just to kill them, we wouldn't be here. A couple of Apache helicopters would just swoop in and clean them up."

When they climbed out of the arroyo, they crouched behind a cluster of boulders and slipped off their heavy backpacks. The wind kicked up, blowing dust across the desert. KD pushed up her night vision goggles, got out a pair of binoculars and focused in on the well-lit hacienda in the near distance. It looked like a traditional adobe building, with a long porch and a red tile roof, even though research indicated it had been built five years ago. It was surrounded by chain-link fencing with security cameras at the corners. A BMW SUV, a Range Rover, a Hummer, and two crew cab pickup trucks were parked in front, but no one was in the yard.

KD handed the binoculars to Blunt. "What do you think?"

He studied the building. "Security team is sitting in an office drinking coffee and watching the monitors."

"So we've got the three cartel leaders. They were each allowed to bring two bodyguards. That's nine total."

"Plus the boss guaranteeing the meet and his security team. That's another six."

"The cooks and the gardener would have gone to bed a long time ago."

Blunt handed the binoculars back to KD. "See that little rock outcropping to our right? That's where I'm going to set up with the sniper rifle."

KD nodded. "I'll move around to the left. Set up in the depression behind that scraggily tree. I'll try to keep moving left once we get this party started."

Blunt pulled the rifle case from his pack, assembled the rifle, and inserted a magazine. "Wouldn't it be something if we could snatch all three of these guys?"

"We'll be lucky to grab Juarez. Even out here in the middle of nowhere we won't have much time before backup arrives."

"Good hunting."

"Same to you, brother."

Blunt scurried across the open ground to the cover of the rocks.

KD waited until he was in place before she crept to the depression next to the spindly tree. The first problem was the fence and the security. She took the RPG-7 rocket launcher from her pack as well as a case that contained three rockets. She loaded the first rocket into the launcher, crouched beside the tree with the launcher on her shoulder, and tapped her comms with her free hand. "Ready?"

"Ready."

The wind gusted from the east, swirling sand up in front of the hacienda. If the wind caught the fins on the rocket, it would turn off course. KD took a breath and waited. The sand settled. She aimed at the BMW SUV and fired. The SUV exploded, shrapnel turning the rest of the vehicles into burning scrap and the chain-link fence into roiled ribbons. She heard the report of the sniper rifle and breaking glass. Three men rushed out of the side of the hacienda in a V formation.

She heard Blunt on the comms. "I see them." He dropped the men in quick succession and turned back to firing through the windows.

KD loaded the second rocket. Now to control their movements. She fired at the right side of the house, but the wind gusted up as she squeezed the trigger. The rocket's fins spun and the rocket turned off course farther right, slamming into the corner of the building. Fucking wind. Still, roof tiles rained into the yard and the front wall of the house collapsed. Two women in nightgowns and a shirtless man ran away from the house into the night.

Bullets started buzzing in from her right, hitting the base of the tree. She tapped her comms. "Gunfire on my two o'clock."

"Two guys behind the busted-up Range Rover," Blunt replied. "I'll try to drive them out."

KD set down the RPG-7 and shouldered her AR-15. The smoke from the fires made it difficult to see what was happening at the wreck of the Ranger Rover. There was a tiny flash. A bullet thudded into the tree by her head. She aimed for an opening where she thought the flash had come from and squeezed the trigger twice. Then she heard the sniper rifle bark.

Blunt was on comms. "You got him to jump. One down."

A helicopter swooped in from the north, its blades chopping the air and raising more dust.

"The chopper wasn't in the briefing."

"Well, it's here now."

KD reached for the rocket launcher and loaded the last rocket. A bullet thudded into the dirt by her knee. She turned toward the helicopter, raised the rocket to her shoulder, and fired. A sharp gust caught the rocket, pulling it to the right, and it slipped by the helicopter and exploded in the air. The helicopter shuddered and took shrapnel but managed to land in the side yard. Mr. Juarez and the other two cartel leaders ran out into the yard, surrounded by seven men who were firing automatic rifles, dust whirling around them. KD fired on the men.

Blunt put three rounds through the plexiglass windshield of the helicopter. Then he dropped one of the men in the yard.

"Cover me." KD jumped up and zigzagged toward the hacienda, firing as she came. The man from behind the Range Rover popped up. KD dove to the ground and rolled, bullets buzzing over her head. She fired a short burst, but the man ducked behind the Range Rover, and she missed.

She scrambled to her feet, still running toward the Range Rover. The man popped up again. Blunt put him down.

"You okay?"

She crawled behind a wrecked truck. "I'm good. I've got the area between the door and the chopper covered."

The nine remaining men were huddled around the door to the helicopter, firing on Blunt. He lay down in the rocks and wriggled backward to safety, bullets buzzing over him like angry wasps.

Three of the men crawled under the helicopter. When they started to come up on the other side, KD reached into the cargo pocket of her pants for a hand grenade, pulled the pin, tossed it toward them, and ducked behind the truck. The explosion knocked them down and damaged the undercarriage of the helicopter. The six on the other side ran from the damaged helicopter, firing a barrage of bullets as they moved back toward the building. KD tossed another hand grenade. The helicopter started burning.

KD tapped her comms. "Is Juarez still alive?"

"I think so."

Blunt, repositioned on the right side of the outcropping, shot two of the men. As soon as they shifted around into KD's sights, she shot another. The last three huddled near the burning helicopter. Flames shot up. They rushed for the side door to the hacienda and Blunt picked off the last two guards. Mr. Juarez tossed his pistol and raised his hands.

KD and Blunt both ran to the burning helicopter. "On the ground," KD said.

Juarez laid down. KD zip-tied his wrists behind his back. Blunt pulled three laminated photos from his jacket and compared the faces to the dead men. "Here's the other two," Blunt said.

KD took photos of them with her smartphone and uploaded them. Then she opened a fingerprinting app and took their thumbprints.

Tina replied via text message. *Positive ID.*

Blunt pulled Juarez to his feet. "Cooperate and you won't die along the way."

Blunt hurried back to the boulders by the arroyo, pushing Juarez along ahead of him. KD went back to the scraggily tree to retrieve the RPG launcher. Then they put on their packs and made their way back down the trail to the spot on a cattle path where they'd left their Suburban. The edge of the sun was just rising in the east.

They put duct tape over Juarez's mouth and a bag over his head before they helped him into the cargo space, zip-tied his ankles and covered him with a blanket. Then they put their gear into the back seat and changed out of their tactical clothes. KD made an encrypted call on her phone. "Got the package. On the move."

"I'm tracking you via your GPS coordinates," Tina replied.

Near an airstrip outside of Nuevo Laredo in the early morning, they pulled over on the side of the road behind a Toyota Highlander with New Mexico plates. Two men, military haircuts and casual clothes, got out.

"Cargo's in the back, gentlemen," KD said.

The men got into the Suburban and drove off toward the airstrip.

KD and Blunt drove into Nuevo Laredo in the Highlander. At the US border, they were waved through the priority lane. In Laredo, Texas, they drove straight to the airport. A middle-age woman dressed in traveling clothes waved at them as they were driving down the passenger drop-off lane. They pulled over. She handed them airline tickets. "Your flight to Dallas/Fort Worth leaves in twenty minutes. Then you've got an hour layover to Reagan National."

"Thanks," KD said.

The woman drove off in the Highlander. KD and Blunt hustled through airport security and got to their gate as the airplane was boarding.

KD plopped down in her seat. "So far, so good."

Blunt sat down beside her. "So far, so good? What have you got? Two bruises and some scuff marks? That job went off like clockwork."

"Where do you think they took our package?"

"Not to the US, that's for sure. They're going to take their time wringing him out. The next few weeks anything they can get out of him is gold."

"We've got some days off coming. What're you going to do?"

"Maybe me and the wife will go fishing."

"You're some kind of romantic, Blunt."

"You must not know anything about fishing. What about you? You got any plans?"

"I don't know. Frank left me a couple of messages on my personal phone."

"What about your new guy?"

"That didn't work out."

"Thought you two went out a few times."

"Just once."

"You look a little down, Doc."

"Just coming off the adrenaline rush."

"Still don't think regular life has much to offer?"

"Still a little hard figuring out my life when I'm not working."

"You don't want to be that adrenaline junky hiding in their apartment between deployments. That doesn't go to a good place."

"Tell me about it."

Blunt bumped his shoulder into hers. "You still haven't come over to the house for supper."

"You inviting me now?"

"Maybe I am."

"What about your romantic fishing trip?"

"What kind of messages does Frank leave? Is he all lovey-dovey or is it straight up sexting?"

"Is that the kind of question you ask your daughter?"

"She better not be sexting or sending naked pictures neither."

KD shook her head and smiled. "I thought you were the expert on young adults."

"I didn't say I was the expert. I just said I had to deal with them. My wife, she's the expert."

"I'm glad we settled that."

"So you bringing Frank when you come to dinner?"

"Maybe."

"Great. I'll talk to the wife. Start working on a date."

A NOTE FROM THE AUTHOR

Thanks for reading *Murder at Mercy Creek*. If you enjoyed it, please post a short review on a review site of your choice. A few words will do. Honest reviews are the number one way I attract new readers.

Thanks so much.

I'd love to hear from you. You can reach me at my website: https://michaelpking.org

ALSO BY MICHAEL P. KING

The KD Thorne Thrillers

The Hunt for the Hijacked Nerve Agent

Murder at Mercy Creek

The Travelers

The Double Cross: A Travelers Prequel

The Traveling Man: Book One

The Computer Heist: Book Two

The Blackmail Photos: Book Three

The Freeport Robbery: Book Four

The Kidnap Victim: Book Five

The Murder Run: Book Six

The Casino Switcheroo: Book Seven

Thicker Than Thieves: Book Eight

The Dark Web Scam: Book Nine

www.ingramcontent.com/pod-product-compliance
Lightning Source LLC
Chambersburg PA
CBHW022116170626
46808CB00002B/748